Tami Rasmussen has captured the essence of mountain life in southern Appalachia with an exciting story that keeps you turning pages until the very end.

—Mary Quigley
Founder, Juliets' book club

"I started reading Murmur one cloudy afternoon, and couldn't put it down til I was finished. Tami Rasmussen's detail to mountain living is awesome, with a great twist!"

Sheree Lynn-Cates

"I didn't see it coming! Exciting and suspenseful! It feels like your in the story, and the characters are wonderful. I can't wait for another one!"

Patricia K. Hodgins

MURMUR

TAMI RASMUSSEN

MURMUR

TATE PUBLISHING
AND ENTERPRISES, LLC

Published by Tate Publishing & Enterprises, LLC
127 E. Trade Center Terrace | Mustang, Oklahoma 73064 USA
1.888.361.9473 | www.tatepublishing.com

Tate Publishing is committed to excellence in the publishing industry. The company reflects the philosophy established by the founders, based on Psalm 68:11,
"The Lord gave the word and great was the company of those who published it."

Book design copyright © 2013 by Tate Publishing, LLC. All rights reserved.
Author photo by Rhonda Callahan-Parrish
Cover design by Rolly Galon
Interior design by Deborah Toling

Published in the United States of America

ISBN: 978-1-62746-871-8
1. Fiction / Mystery & Detective / General
2. Fiction / Action & Adventure
13.08.08

Dawn Lynn
1940-2008

CHAPTER ONE

Today I wake up with an uneasy feeling in the pit of my stomach, and my mind is positively racing. I have a hunch there is something really bad going to happen today, and my anxiety is already rearing its ugly head. I get these suspicious inklings on countless occasions. They're not premonitions like a psychic or something, it's just a real gut feeling. The scariest problem is more times than not, something will actually happen to prove my hunch.

I try to stop my impulse to worry. "Sonny Branch, whatever is gonna happen will happen, and it's out of your dang control!" I can talk myself out of these disquieting thoughts sometimes, but it's mostly a futile exercise. The mountain gap I live in can lend itself to a lot of isolation durin' the winter months. Sometimes it can be hard to differentiate between truth, fiction, or self-induced paranoia.

I have seen very few people this winter, and I couldn't make it to town much. Most people think it odd that

I would choose such a life for myself, and there is only one answer. "God created this mountain, and it's by his grace I get to live on it!" I believe to my core that I am truly blessed to live in a countryside that surrounds my life and home with perfection. The beauty of White Rock Mountain drew me to Franklin, North Carolina, back in the early sixties. I love the serenity that the mountain and Hickory Gap offers up to me every day. I wouldn't trade any of it for all the money in the world.

The mornings on White Rock Mountain are picturesque and animated. I gaze out the partially open bedroom window and watch nature convene as a new day begins. The sun is shining on this cool March morning, illuminating the brilliant Carolina sky. Except for the occasional murmurs from distant birds squabbling, this mornin' is oddly quiet and motionless. I glance over at a nearby calendar, and I can't believe that it is already March 1. We can still expect snow, but spring is right around the corner. I'm quickly jolted out of my thoughts when out of the blue I hear footsteps running up the front stairs. Whoever it is approaches the front door.

There is a series of timid knocks, and I hear a soft-spoken voice. "Sonny, are you home?"

It's my neighbor Iris Bell, and she sounds genuinely worried. Not caring about my appearance or apparel I jump out of bed and run to answer the door. "Iris, what the heck is the matter?"

She's obviously in distress, but promptly articulates her crisis. "I'm so glad your home. Anna went into active labor early yesterday evening, and she may be in trouble. Her water broke several hours ago, but there is still very little progress. Her temperature is goin' up, and I'm afraid infection may set in. I desperately need your help. Can you come and give me a hand?"

"We've been expecting the baby to arrive any day now, but we've been preparing for the birth over the past several months. Did you send someone after Doctor Cooper?"

She quickly answers. "I sent one of the guys to go and fetch him. He should be on his way. Please hurry, I'm extremely concerned."

Iris and her live-in Peter Benjamin own a large parcel of land just north of mine but farther up the mountain gap. They operate a shared collective farm called "Why Worry." The farm produces fruits, veggies, raw milk, honey, and a whole variety of goods that the resident farmers and artisans sell to the public. I ain't never heard of a "collective farm," before meetin' Iris, and to me it is more of a working sixties type hippie commune. Iris and Peter offer all passersby a hot meal and a place to lay their head at Why Worry. On any given day there can be any number of folks staying at the farm. The breathtaking views attract a lot of hippies and other interesting characters to Hickory Gap. Typically they make the trek on foot. Most of the folks rely on the kindness of strangers to pick them up hitchhikin' and have only the belongings they can manage to carry. Current and future potential inhabitants of Why Worry arrive from different places and situations, but their commonalities are much more interrelated than one may think. The community at Why Worry is searching and pining for people who share their same philosophies, ideologies, and life styles. Iris and Peter yearn for simplicity and a sense of belongin', just like the travelers who seek out their collective farm. I'm sure the residents of Why Worry will never forget their time livin' at the commune.

Iris and Peter are extremely down-to-earth people, and both have big hearts. Iris is pale skinned, blue-eyed, and very red-headed. She is petite and in her twenties. Iris never knew her real parents, and she has no recollection of either of them. They abandoned her when she was three years old, and has never known why or what happened. Growing up she moved from foster home to foster home but never got adopted. When Iris turned sixteen years old, she was given legal permission to live on her own as an adult. Shortly after her emancipation she met Peter Benjamin, and they moved in together almost immediately. Peter is blue-eyed, tan, tall, and has curly blonde hair that falls down to his lower back. He is ten years older than Iris, and anyone can tell they're crazy in love with each other.

Peter was drafted into the Army and spent one tour of duty in Vietnam. He thought about dodging the draft and goin' to Canada. He had second thoughts, and in the end went to Vietnam after all. He was shot a couple of times in a conflict that resulted in hundreds of dead soldiers and civilians. He fought courageously and earned the Silver Star, Purple Heart, and a one-way trip home. The nightly news is wall-to-wall coverage of the wars gruesome details, side by side, with all the anti-war protests that are taking place around our great country. Peter isn't shy about roping you into a political heart-to-heart when he's able. He is a card-carrying liberal democrat and fully prepared to help the cause against the unpopular war.

Iris drives her rusted jeep like an old tank. "Your freaking me out Iris, could you slow down just a little? I feel my ass comin' up off the seat, and I'm gonna fall out!" The doors and roof have been taken off, and I'm holding onto a torn leather strap for dear life. Iris laugh's. "No one has fallen out yet, and it's gonna get a lot worse!" The maze of old logging trails are rugged and getting anywhere on the mountain can be a challenge, even for the best four-wheel drive vehicle. For many mountain families, a home birth is the traditional and preferred way to have their babies goin' back generations. The hospital setting is cold and sterile, and the atmosphere doesn't render the personal experience of a home birth. Likewise; they are also very expensive, and some folks around here can't afford it.

I don't have any formal education beyond the tenth grade. I take every chance I can get to educate myself at the library and read everything I can get my hands on. I've been successful in helping many mountain families have their babies over the years, and I praise God, and his grace that everything turned out well. Iris hits a big ol' pothole, and jerks me out of my thoughts. "Youngin' will you please watch out!" After what seems like an hour, we finally approach the entrance to Why Worry. I can suddenly hear the bustle of a working community. Voices are chattering with excitement, and traditional blue grass music is playing in the distance.

Many of the people who live in this charming commune play music and sing. There are a variety of guitars, fiddles, banjos, mandolins, and my personal favorite, the dulcimer. The days at Why Worry are alive with activity. When the sun begins to set on the mountain I can hear the happiness of music and singing come all the way down the holler and into my open windows. The wonderful sounds lull me to sleep at night. The music is as diverse as the people who live here. They are amazing musicians and artists, but most importantly they are all farmers.

We pass Iris and Peter's home place on our way to Luke and Anna's. "Man, you guys sure have a pretty log cabin! All your hard work paid off, and the teepee still looks spectacularly cool!" Western North Carolina is steeped in Cherokee Indian culture and history. It's one of the reasons Iris and Peter fell in love with this location. They built a traditional Indian teepee with the assistance of a few local experts from nearby Cherokee, North Carolina. Iris and Peter were bound and determined to live in a teepee. The teepee and White Rock expose beautiful pictures and memories for all of us, but after two long cold winters livin' in it, Iris, had enough. "It was hard livin' for sure, but Peter and me loved every minute of it!" She lasted longer than I would have thought. I can't help myself, "I'm surprised you're not the one knocked up?" She sheepishly smiles in response. It was pretty darn neat though, and I will always cherish the endless hours sitting around the campfire and sharing stories. Those were fun times for sure.

After a considerable amount of hard work and a whole lot of personal conviction, Iris and Peter built a stunning hand hewn log cabin. They collected and prepared all of their logs during the two years they lived in the teepee. "Ya' know Peter always said buildin' our own log cabin was a true labor of love, but anyone who's done it will tell you its well worth it when you're finished." I'm talking over the noisy ride, "Well, ya'll did a really great job. Sure wasn't any easy thing to do." Iris and Peter love to share the memories of those two years with anyone who will lend them an ear, and for me the stories never grow old. Their lives are unfussy, plain, and they live comfortably. Peter and Iris believe Why Worry is their fate and destiny, and the idea of a commune appealed to both of them. "Peter and me couldn't imagine livin' anywhere else! We're almost there. Ain't the place changed a lot since you been here last?" Iris concentrates on driving, and I concentrate on holdin' on for dear life. "Yeah, a few more rocks in the road than I remember!" We both break out laughing.

White Rock Mountain and Hickory Gap gives all of our lives a profound sense of stability unparalleled to anything or anywhere else. The collective farm is working out really great these first few years and has surpassed Iris and Peter's expectations. The hippies and transients passing through are mostly non-violent pacifists just like Iris and Peter. Occasionally a few problems will arise, but it is always handled peaceably. Everyone that resides on the mountain shares a great respect and admiration for one another, and the folks at Why Worry won't tolerate any kind of trouble. Why Worry and White Rock Mountain represent all that is beautiful about the Southern Appalachian Mountains of Franklin, North Carolina, in 1975.

There isn't any electricity or telephone service accessible to Hickory Gap, and all of us who live here prefer it this way. I read a lot to pass the time and have a perfectly functionin' outhouse. I catch rainwater and use a homemade portable shower put together with a bucket, rope, and garden hose. The creek supplies the rest of my water. I prefer to live off the grid, and my lifestyle does not require much money.

I was born and raised in Omaha, Nebraska, and moved to North Carolina in 1962. I found work at a local sewin' factory when I first arrived here. I didn't have any manufacturing skills, and the whole experience was quite interesting. I didn't really get along with all the "cackling hens" that worked there, so I pretty much kept to myself. I enjoyed listening to the nightly soap opera on the radio. The ongoing story made the tediousness of sewing go much faster. It didn't take long before I realized that I just wasn't cut out to work in a factory. I decided to try and sell my artwork at local art shows for income. I love to paint, but my passion is writin'. It's worked out pretty good so far, and I have inspirational scenery all around me to replicate. I've sold several paintings, and I am currently workin' on my very first fictional novel. I would never breathe it out loud, but I secretly dream of being a best selling novelist one day.

Iris turns the jeep onto an old pig trail that leads us to a small and very primitive cabin. "Here we are!" I hadn't ever seen the place, so I wasn't real sure what to expect. The trees and tall grass strike us as we pass by, and suddenly we start to hear the sounds of a woman giving birth.

Iris shouts. "Hold on, Sonny!" We slide sideways in the mud, and I quickly grab onto what ever I can to brace myself. "Holy crap! Are you kiddin' me?" Iris skillfully swerves the jeep, stopping within inches of the diminutive shack where the impending birth is about to finally take place. Once the jeep finally comes to a complete stop, Iris and I jump out at the same time. "I'm a gettin' to ol' for adventure rides lil' missy! My butt's drawed up to the size of a pea!" I'm stretching to work out the kinks, and Iris doesn't even slow down. "Quit complainin' ol' lady, and come on!" Through the open front door I can see Peter, along with the other men, sitting vigil in the living room. They stop talking long enough to motion us in the house, and towards the bedroom. The left over early morning heat from the wood stove is stifling. There are windows open, but it gives me little comfort or relief. When we enter Anna's bedroom, I see her husband, Luke, is at the bedside wiping her forehead with a cool, wet cloth. His voice is controlled and hushed, and he is talking to her in a very loving way. "You're doing great Anna! Iris is back with Sonny, and were gonna have this baby." The room is quiet other than Luke's whispered reassurances. He's trying his level best to keep her focused and calm. Luke is visibly nervous, but does a good job hiding it from Anna. I take Anna's hand. "Lil' mama try not to push until I tell you to." "I can't do it no more, Sonny! It hurts! It hurts real bad! I need this baby out!" "Anna you concentrate, and listen to what I'm sayin'. Take deep breaths just like you practiced. Luke help her out." She does not want to push prematurely, but the urge is becoming too overbearing. It is only by pure determination and strength that she can hold off until the proper time to start. Iris moves quickly throughout the room picking up bits of information on Anna's condition while she was gone.

Anna and Luke came to Why Worry about four months ago. They look to be closer in age to Iris than Peter. The pregnancy was already several months along when they asked permission to stay on long term at the farm. They both love the mountains, and hope to raise their baby in the commune. There was never any question what the answer to Luke and Anna's question was going to be, and we have been preparing for this day ever since Iris and Peter agreed to let them stay on at Why Worry. This is Luke and Anna's first baby, and it is also officially the first baby to be born at Why Worry.

I always thought that Iris and Peter would be the first to have children, but Iris isn't quite ready to jump in headfirst. Anna's pregnancy has been picture perfect up until now. She is young and healthy, so neither Iris nor I have been too concerned. She's had regular visits with a local doctor in Franklin for her maternity care, and there haven't been any indications of potential problems.

"How long ago did ya'll send for Doc Cooper?" Luke quickly responds. "I sent a couple of the fellers in my ol' truck to go fetch him an hour or so ago? They should be here anytime?" "We didn't see 'em on the road comin' up!" Doc Cooper is a family doctor that was born in these mountains. He came back to Franklin and set up his practice after graduating from medical school. He is seventy-four years young and has practiced in Macon county for forty some odd years. Dr. Cooper is well respected and has delivered a lot of babies at home in these mountains. He is one of the few remaining doctors that will still do house calls. Lucky for us he has agreed to assist in Anna's home delivery if we need him.

I look around the room, and then at Iris. I recognize one or two of the women here to help out, but don't know any names. They all politely nod their heads in acknowledgement. No one is speaking, and you can feel tension permeating the room. They've been helping Iris and Anna for several hours, and all of them are very anxious to get this baby out. I look over and see all of the supplies we will need present on a small table in the corner. I purchased plastic clamps at the hardware store. Someone has sterilized them, and when the time comes I will use one to clamp the umbilical cord. Stacks of clean towels are ready to use when the baby is born, along with other assorted things that we may need.

The room is naturally warm, and with all the activity and people present to assist there is no need for any additional heat. March can be cold, but thank goodness today is mild. We are all anxious for a favorable outcome and are eager to get this baby born. The last stage of labor has taken an extra long time, and both Iris and I are concerned. Our only saving grace is that Dr. Cooper is on his way. Luke and Anna both divert their attention from the important task at hand to express their appreciation to me for coming to help. I squeeze Luke's shoulder. "Thanks for comin' to help Sonny. I've been real nervous!" "I know you have youngin'. I know you have. You're doin' a great job!" I take Anna's hand, "How ya doing mama?" "Gettin' tired Sonny! Gettin' real tired! I just want it over." I look around the room with a reassuring attitude and say a quick prayer out loud. "Dear Lord, please keep this youngin' and her baby safe. I ask for your guidance, a quick delivery, and a healthy baby. Amen." After several amen's from everyone in the room, I take a deep breath and get ready. Underneath I'm scared as heck, but I don't want anyone to know it. I take one last glance at Iris, and she returns my obvious concern with a cautious smile.

I position myself on a stool at the foot of the bed in front of Anna. After a brief observation, I can see the baby's head starting to crown. "The baby is comin'! I can see a head full of hair! Look Luke!" Anna is relieved, "Luke, can you see our baby? Is there a lot of hair?" Astonished at what he is witnessing, Luke joyfully exclaims, "Yes! Yes! Tons of black hair!" Iris assesses Anna's progress, and her gaurded smile relaxes. "Why hell fire girl, you've been busy since I left!" Anna returns the lighthearted sentiment with a weary smile. Relief replaces my trepidation with the progress that Anna has made on her own in the short time that it took Iris to fetch me. We place an antique dressing mirror at the end of the bed so both Anna and Luke can watch the miracle of their baby's birth. I help place Luke and Anna's hands on their baby's crowning head, so they can feel the hair for themselves. "See, see, check it out you guys! Ain't it cool as all get out! That's the very top of your baby's head!" Everyone can see the miracle of birth unfolding in the beautiful antique mirror. Grand smiles return to both their faces as they gently stroke the top of their baby's head. Tears stream down Luke's face. "Oh my God! Anna can ya see it? That's our baby!" Anna unable to speak prepares for another contraction coming on.

"Let's get this done! Iris, hand me the bottle of mineral oil sitting on the bureau." I explain to Anna what I'm going to do next and pour a generous amount of the oil around the baby's crowning head. "The mineral oil is gonna keep your skin from tearing as the baby comes out." I speak confidently and calmly. "Anna, Luke, hopefully we can get the baby out in one good push!" I ask Iris to assist me. "Iris, will you help get Anna's legs into position, and please monitor her contractions?" Iris places her hand at the top portion of Anna's stomach. When a contraction comes, Iris will be able to feel the muscle tightening and let us know when it's time for Anna to push.

Luke is standing behind Anna's shoulders and helping to support her back. She is in a great position to help push out this baby, and the look on her face is one of great resolve. I look around the room, and again at Iris, Luke, and Anna. "Anna, when you feel your stomach tightening, it will be time to push! Iris, let me know when you feel the contraction starting. All right everybody, let's have us a baby!"

There is a cool, calm, and collected silence in the room. Within seconds, Iris and Anna confirm to one another and me that a contraction is on the way. "All right Sonny, I feel her stomach tightening up."

I look reassuringly at Anna. "Let's do it again. Take a deep breath, and when I tell you to, push down hard!" Following all my instructions, Anna takes a deep breath and gets into position. Luke helps her get ready. "All right, push!"

She begins to push down hard.

"Keep going, keep going, and keep pushing!"

She exhales and screams. "I can't do it any more!"

I look at Iris, and she confirms the contraction hasn't ended yet. In a loving but very firm voice I coach Anna to finish her contraction. "Honey, I need you to take another deep breath, and push as hard as you can!"

Anna's immense determination, and every last ounce of energy she possessed, pushes the baby's head out with the labor pain. She collapses in exhaustion and relief. Luke's gaze is mesmerized on the baby's protruding head, and he is praising Anna for her hard work and perseverance.

I quickly suction out the unborn baby's mouth and nose before the next contraction comes. The unborn infant screams out with a lusty cry, and a great sigh of relief fills the room. Tears stream down Luke's face. His look of amazement tells the whole story of the experience unfolding before his eyes.

I can't imagine what it must feel like. There is purity in the birth of a baby that parallels nothin' else in life, and it must be very powerful when parents see their child for the first time. There is such an awe and respect for a women's body that men truly come to understand when they experience the birth of their children.

The pulsating umbilical cord is loosely wrapped around the baby's neck, but thankfully it is easy to remove. Iris quickly speaks up. "We're havin' another contraction! I feel it comin'!" Anna and Luke are ready, and everyone prepares for the baby to make its majestic appearance.

The hard-fought contraction does not deliver the infant as expected. Anna's pushing is good, but she can't seem to move the baby down and out of the birth canal. My first thought is the baby's shoulder could be stuck. This difficulty can cause grave problems for the baby. We must get this baby out as quickly as possible! I look at Iris, and mouth the words "shoulder maybe stuck?"

Iris nods back. "Could very well be."

I ask Emily, one of the girls in the room, to help us. I don't want to scare everyone. I coolly explain to Emily that the baby's shoulder may be stuck, and what I will need her to help us do. "I need you to climb up on the bed, and when she has another contraction please use both of your hands to help push out this baby." I show her exactly where to thrust on Anna's stomach when the time comes. Emily quickly jumps up on the bed, places her hands where I instructed, and is prepared to help. I ask someone to send a truck out to see what's holdin' up Doc Cooper. He can't be to far away. My only concern is the guys aren't able to find him.

I survey the room and all the faces. A contraction is starting, and we need to deliver this baby. "All right, everyone, here we go again. "I learned from years of experience that you can manually apply pressure on the abdomen in a specific area during the contraction, and this may help the shoulders pass through. My unease is the great possibility of fracturing one or both of the baby's shoulders. In an emergency it is better to break the shoulder than to risk the life of the child.

Anna exclaims, "Here comes another one!"

I look around. "Okay, okay, is everyone ready?" I return my attention to the baby. "Anna, bend your legs up toward your chest, and hold onto your thighs. Luke and Iris, please help her. Anna, push this baby out!" I grit my teeth and hold my own breath. I find myself pushing with her contraction.

By the grace of God there is good progress, and the baby moves down some. The infant's eyes are still open and alert. "Keep pushing, Anna! Emily, apply pressure to her stomach now!" She pushes on her stomach exactly where I showed her with a straight downward motion. "Press a little bit more Emily!" At long last the shoulders pass, and I can easily guide the newborn out onto the clean towels waiting to catch the infant.

I can hardly contain my excitement. "It's a girl!" A beautiful new human enters the world. Suddenly the delightful cry of a newborn permeates the room and the house. Loud exhales, and heaps of joyous sentiments break the intense silence. Delight replaces the look of trepidation on Anna and Luke's faces. The baby doesn't breathe on its own until we cut the umbilical cord, so I quickly clamp the cord in two places. The quicker we can cut the cord the better off the baby will be.

I hand the scissors to Luke, and he cuts the cord between the two clamps exactly where I show him. "Good job, Luke!"

Iris promptly places the baby girl on Anna's bare chest and stomach. She vigorously rubs the baby down with the dry towels. I suction her mouth and nose robustly with a bulb syringe, and after a few minutes of hearty stimulation the baby's ashen color quickly changes to pink. She is able to move both of her arms, so luckily we didn't cause a fracture. Her breathing shows no signs of distress, and she is very alert.

Luke and Anna name her Paisley.

Emily helps me get her measurements, and I am very pleased with her weight. "Good weight, you guys!"

Iris tends to Anna's postpartum care while I thoroughly check over baby Paisley to make sure everything looks normal. Dr. Cooper will be here soon. He will do a complete examination of both his patients and will also do the required paperwork necessary for Luke and Anna to get Paisley's birth certificate.

The atmosphere in the room is so joyful, and everyone is in great spirits. Luke cannot be prouder of his two girls. Flashbulbs are going off everywhere, and Anna is recovering great so far. After a vigorous and quick exam, I place Paisley back on Anna's chest, skin to skin.

Instinctively little Paisley begins bobbing her head up and down searching for her mother's breast to suckle. Anna proudly latches Paisley onto her breast with minimal help. She has a good suck, and Anna will do a fine job breastfeeding. Iris and I look at each other with tears in our eyes, and with the great satisfaction of a job well done. It is a truly pleasing ending.

I give Anna and Luke some last minute instructions regarding the care of both Paisley and Anna before we head back down the gap.

Iris and I hop into the jeep and head back to my place. I close my eyes tight during the ride home and give thanks to God for helping me find this place and these people. We pass the doctor, and give him an update on Anna and Paisley's condition. Iris and I both feel better knowing he's on his way. It seems like only a minute, and we arrive at the turn off to my driveway.

When we crest the last curve at the top of my winding gravel drive way, two large poplar trees frame White Rock perfectly. Carolina blue skies and White Rock Mountain still takes my breath away every time I see it. Each season in the Great Smoky Mountains is awe-inspiring, and we love to celebrate all of them. I can see my best friend, Riley Stone, sitting on the front porch waiting for me to get home.

Iris abruptly stops the jeep just inches away from the bottom of the steps. I felt sure she was going to plow right into my stairs, but she didn't. She grabs me into a great big hug before I can get out the door. "Thank you so much, Sonny Branch!"

I hug her back. "Iris, I'm so glad that it all worked out." I close my eyes for just a split second, and I can see the little shack. I think to myself about the miracle of Paisley's birth. "You know, Iris, a small house can hold a lot of love." I can sense a change has come over Iris. Like a sadness? "Come on in and let an ol' lady make you a fresh pot of coffee to celebrate a job well done. Don't pay no mind to Riley, she can wait." "Yeah, I'll take ya' up on that offer. Sounds great! I could surely use it!"

CHAPTER TWO

At this moment Riley doesn't have a happy look on her face. She jumps up abruptly and meets me halfway down the steps. That nagging gut instinct from this morning is starting to bug me again. "Hey, what's up chick? You missed out on baby Paisley's birthday. Iris and I were just gonna make some coffee to celebrate. It was totally far out." Iris says, "Far out alright! The dang shoulder got stuck, and Sonny thought she was gonna have to break it to get the baby out!"

Riley and I became close friends years ago. She was born and raised in Franklin not far from here. She befriended me shortly after I moved to White Rock back in the early sixties. We are both in our early forties now, and neither of us ever married or had any kids. When we talk Riley always has the same complaint, "I can never find a man that works as hard as I do!"

That's probably the real absolute truth of it! I can't help but smile wildly at the thought. She is maybe all of five foot and four inches tall. She has coal black hair, and wears it super short like a boy. She is in great physical condition and is a charming somebody with a very strong personality. Riley Stone is traditional, hard working, and still believes that a handshake is a gesture of honor and respect. Johnny Stone, her daddy, set the example for Riley growing up. He was a tough man, but fair, and he loves his little girl.

The Stone family has a long history of logging in Macon County. When Johnny turned thirteen he started working for his daddy, and he logged Hickory Gap back in around 1914. He battled deadly mountain rattlers and copperheads logging this land, and his pay was a meager ten cents a day. To this day Mr. Stone is still jumpy about the snakes when he occasionally comes to visit me at the cabin. I can't help but mess with him. He doesn't appreciate the humor. "Sonny Branch, you ain't right! You just wait till you come up on one." Unfortunately he lost half of his left arm in a horrific logging accident shortly after his sixteenth birthday. Family and friends still say he is lucky to be alive. The accident never stopped him from loggin' or raisin' Riley.

Riley's mom passed on from cancer when Riley was just a young girl, and Johnny raised her best he could. Her mother and father both come from large mountain families that go back generations in Macon County. There is standing room only when her family comes out to the funeral home. It wasn't long ago one of the churches down on Tessentee was holding funeral services, and the whole entire floor caved in. All due to the enormous crowd that showed up to pay their final respects. It was no surprise to me when Riley told me that it was one of her relative's funerals. My family is minuscule compared to hers, but Riley has assured me that her family will gladly fill the church pews at my funeral. She always has a plan, and I love that about her.

The woman cuts her own wood, hunts, and has lived in these mountains her whole life. She's an only child and just like a sister to me. Riley's fashion and demeanor is of a tomboy rather than a lady. She is currently dressed in an old pair of blue jeans, and a torn t-shirt that has long passed its good days. I can't even read the writin' on it any more. I pass her on the steps and snigger to myself. She follows close on my heels as I walk up to the front door. I can hear huffing under her breath. She makes this annoying noise when she is really upset over somethin'. I love her, but sometimes she thinks that nothin' else exists outside of her own bubble.

"Riley, Riley, what could possibly be more important then Anna and Luke's brand new baby girl, Paisley?" I am gettin' annoyed. "Riley, please stop huffin' under your breath, it drives me crazy." I can tell she wants to get something off of her chest, but when we get inside I tell her. "Not now! Somethin's up with Iris." Riley looks at Iris and calms down. Iris grabs a squat, and quietly waits for the coffee. I fiddle around in the kitchen, and I finally her open up about what's buggin' her. "I can't stop thinkin' about my ma! What could've possibly been so bad that she would leave me? I don't get it ya'll? After what I seen today, I just can't believe any mom could just give away there kid?" I had no idea how profoundly the birth affected Iris, and her emotions are running at an all time high. This is the first time I've seen the youngin' so tore up over her ma. Sure, she said things, but I ain't never heard her really talk so personally 'bout it. "Do ya' think about her a lot?" "All the time! I wonder what she looks like, and how she smells? I think about everything that I would love to tell her. So many questions that I want to ask her." Riley is unbelievably restrained from comment, and sits quietly. I know she is busting to tell us something, but she also realizes that Iris is havin' a melt down. Riley never could resist a good melt down. Iris can't hold back the tears any longer. "My life could've been so different. My whole existence could've been different!" I hug her tight. "But Iris, it could've been different in a bad way? Sweetie you don't know what it would've been like? It might have been awful, and with or without her you have a great life now!" Riley adds her words of wisdom. "No would'ves, could'ves, or should'ves that's what I'm sayin'!" She is hell bent on getting something off of her chest, and she won't let it rest until she does. "We're gonna have new neighbors! I found out today that outsiders just purchased a several hundred acre tract of White Rock Mountain land starting at the beginning of Hickory Gap Road!" Iris and I look at her stunned. "Oh, and that ain't all! Someone bought a small piece of land up your way too Iris. From what I gather several small plots of land have been bought up by all kinda of people. What the heck! This ain't no neighborhood!"

In disbelief, I ask her to repeat to me what she just said. I want to make sure that I am hearing her right. "Come again? Did ya just say hundreds of acres?" "Yep, hundreds of acres sold! Don't that beat all?"

We all notice Daniel Calabash standing at the open front door ready to knock moments after Riley divulges the news. Everyone in these parts call him by his nick name, Stash. He got the name cause he likes to smoke a lot of pot. In all the commotion and excitement we didn't hear him come up the steps. He overheard Riley through the screen door, and I can tell by the look on his face this news does not make him happy. I motion him into the house to join us. "Hey, Stash! Come on in."

My neighbor and good friend, Stash and I are the original residents of White Rock Mountain. Iris and Peter came later. He has lived on White Rock longer than any of us. He is a mountain man and patriot. Unlike the anger and resentment that Peter harbors, Daniel Calabash is very proud of his service to our country during this heartbreaking Vietnam War. I'm a libertarian, so I get along with both of them. Stash moved to White Rock several years before joining the Marines. He calls it his very own "parcel of paradise." The land really belongs to his lifelong buddy Scott, who is still overseas fighting in the war. Stash lives in an old camper truck and collects all of his water from a small branch that runs through the property. The kitchen is located outside under a large green army tarp. It consists of a grill, fire pit, Coleman stove, coolers, and a table. The bathroom is out in nature. The winters are harsh livin' in a camper. He makes due and doesn't complain 'cause he loves this land. He would tell me all the time. "This is the closest thing to nirvana as I could ever imagine findin' in this life time."

Stash walks in the door. His voice is low and resonating as he asks, "So what's this I hear about foreigners buyin' up the mountain?" He nudges me with his elbow.

Riley immediately explains to him what she found out at Baxter's feed and seed. He listens carefully and quietly, and I see him getting angrier by the minute. Stash does not like many people around him, and he certainly doesn't like change. Upset by the new revelation, he almost forgets the reason why he's here in the first place. "Oh yeah, I need a ride to town next time someone goes off the mountain." Stash's truck has been out of commission for a few days now.

He got drunk and rolled the truck off into a small ravine goin' home early the other morning. Peter happened to be coming up the gap and caught a glimpse of Stash's truck off the side of the bank. He stopped to see if he was still in the truck. "Hey dude ya down there?" Stash replies, "Yeah man, I'm still down here!" It didn't take long for Peter to climb down the embankment to help him. Stash tells Peter. "I reckon that I've been down there almost eight hours." Stash said he just slept off his drunkenness before trying to climb up the bank. His truck was seriously tore up, but Stash is fine. This ain't the first time he's done it, and lucky for him he wasn't seriously hurt in the smash up. All of us try to watch out for him on the road. We all convinced him a while back to take the camper off his truck if he needs to go off the mountain. It is not good for him to drive around with his house, 'specially if he's drinkin' white liquor. I'm just glad the camper wasn't on his truck when he toddled into the ravine. Thankfully he still has a roof over his head. It was an amusing conversation when we had it, and thank God he listened to our suggestion.

Riley shrugs her shoulders and snaps, "I repeat once again, you guys, over two hundred acres of White Rock Mountain got sold to folks from out of the state!"

Stash thinks foreigners are anyone who don't live on White Rock Mountain, Hickory Gap, or Franklin, which is just about everyone on the planet. We have all feared this day. Over the years we have talked about the possibility, but we just never expected this time would arrive so soon.

Riley always thinks the worst, of course. "Hell fire, ya'll! What if the strangers start buildin' a bunch of houses and turn Hickory Gap into some kinda neighborhood? Oh my God, that would be sickenin'."

None of us ever wanted to see change, and it feels like we got run over by a dump truck. Riley ends our momentary reflection. "What about Why Worry? What if these people don't understand their way of life?"

The vision of people coming to White Rock has important implications to me personally. This means electrical and phone lines will come, and that means more people will come with them. Next they'll want to pave our road, and open up our utopia to everyone. Stash's expression sums it up for all of us, and the disappointment is written all over his face. I expected him to say somethin', but he don't say a word about the news, and politely excuses himself. "Gotta go ladies, I'm burnin' daylight."

I quickly remember before he leaves. "Stash, I'll let 'em all know ya' need a ride to town."

He throws up his hand and waves, acknowledging my remark. He mutters something under his breath as he leaves out the door. Riley and I can still hear him mumbling to himself as he goes down the steps.

"Sonny, he looks like his dog just died." We both watch him leave and begin his unhurried trek back up the mountain before the day gets away. Iris gets up to leave. "Well girls I gotta get back to see how Anna and Paisley are doin'." I hug her great big. "Sorry 'bout your ma. You know everything happens for a reason." Iris hugs Riley too on her way out the door. Iris tired and wore out says, "I hate that folks are comin' to the mountain, but there ain't a thing we can do about it girls. It's been a wild day, and I'm pooped."

The last several weeks since Paisley's birth have been pretty quiet on the mountain, but today President Ford declared the Vietnam War over. Stash wants to party, and word is he's havin' a cookout this evenin' to celebrate the wars end., so we're all gonna hang out at his place later up in the day. Peter has even come, and he's in a celebratory mood. The news is enormous, and we all rejoice the wars end. It has been a while since we all got together at Stash's place. Peter, Iris, and I are sitting outdoors in the kitchen when we see a car coming up Hickory Gap Road.

Stash comes out of his camper to see who it is. "Hey everybody, I bet it's Scott!"

The unfamiliar car pulls in behind the four wheelers that currently litter the gravel road. Stash is clearly excited to see his friend, but quickly realizes that it is not Scott in the car. Two passengers emerge, and Stash sees that it's Scott's parents. He walks towards the car to greet 'em. "Hey you guys! Long time no see. How the heck are ya'll?" They made a special trip to see and talk with Stash personally. Stash reaches out to shake hands with Scotts dad, but instead they hug. "You look good Stash!" "Man, you too Sir!" Scott's mom watches somberly at the exchange. Stash grabs her up. "You look great to ma'am!" We sensed bad news by the look on their faces. We all start to stand up and excuse ourselves from the party so they can have privacy. Stash immediately glances around to each one of us. "I want ya'll to stay. Please you guys stay here." Each of us ease back down into our seats. Stash and Scott's folks join us at the table.

They both comment how pretty this place is and share plenty of hugs and memories. Looking puzzled, Stash questions them about Scott. "I love seeing ya'll but where's Scott? Man, we have some serious catchin' up to do, and I can't wait to crack open a brewsky with 'em."

With tears in their eyes, and obviously very distressed, Scott's dad speaks first. "Stash, in the last days of the war, Scott lost his life." Barely able to get the words out. "My son died a hero and my god he will come home as a hero." Unlike wars in the past, not many people approved of this war, and our returning soldiers may not receive the heroes' welcome they so richly deserve.

His ma is gulping back her tears. "Another soldier will be flying with him home from Vietnam, so he won't travel alone. Should be in the next few days honey? We'll let you know something, just as soon as we know something." That is a great comfort to everyone, but especially to Stash. Visibly weighted down by the dreadful news, Stash is having a hard time during the days leading up to Scott's funeral. He stays drunk and refuses to talk to anyone. Everyone is very concerned about him. We all take turns checking in on him and bring him food.

The day of the funeral has arrived, and personally I'm glad it will be over. I hope Stash can move on from this devastating blow. Riley and I attend the memorial service with him. The service is a grand tribute to a patriot, a good son, and a beloved friend. The church is packed full, and Scott's casket is draped with the American flag. He is buried in a family plot here in Franklin, and the weather cannot have been better. Scott received military honors, a gun salute, and his parents are presented with the flag that covered his casket.

The service was exceptional. Stash had a lot of support and spent a good deal of time with his friends and Scott's family. We briefly attended a wake at Scott's family home before we head back to the mountain. The ride home was long. Stash sits in silence, and even Riley is unusually quiet. I worry about Stash's well being, but feel sure he will mend with time.

Slowly, one by one, the days are passing. The sun rises every morning, and Stash is looking and feeling much better. His spirits are increasing, and every day he's gettin' more energy and strength back. Today he is announcing somethin' very important, and has invited all of us to his humble and incredibly comfortable abode. Everyone gathers in the kitchen, and we're excited to hear the news flash. Stash takes a deep breath. "Scott left me this property! Since his death I have pondered and pondered what to do, and I've made a decision. I'm gonna start buildin' a log cabin right where the camper sits now. It's what he'd want me to do. Rest in peace brother, hoorah!"

Our response is one of joy and excitement. "Way cool Stash! I'll help you with any work ya need done." I clank my cup of coffee with a spoon. "Toast to Stash! Your a great dude, and better friend. Congrats on your new home!" Everyone joins in with their own toasts. It's great to see Stash happy again. Stash is not a young man anymore. The three tours in Vietnam made him very muscular and strong. Lifting logs will be effortless for him. We all watch the log cabin take shape over the next weeks. He spends every waking moment working on it, and he is growing much stronger every day. The American flag flies with great pride at the entrance of his driveway. It honors his best friend and fallen comrades.

Stash is a kind man when he is sober and straight, but he likes his homegrown marijuana and moonshine a lot. Consumed together in large quantities, he sometimes gets a little crazy and aggressive. You just have to put him in his place and choose not to be around him during those times. We all know his heart is heavy. He is a survivor and American hero. The local kids tell stories about him being the hermit who lives on White Rock Mountain, and the stories amuse Stash greatly.

The summer has come and gone surprisingly fast, and without any harsh changes to the mountain. A new home place is going in, and all the heavy equipment used to build the new home has stirred up all the rattlesnake dens. I now understand Riley's daddy's fear of snakes. He always said, "There are some old, old, rattlesnake dens up in these rock tables. You best keep an eye out for 'em, and them ol' copperheads will come outta nowhere. Them's the ones you gotta watch out for." He was right. The mountain rattlers are at every turn now they disrupted the land with bulldozers. Johnny told me that you can tell how old a rattler is by the number of buttons on its tail, and I must have killed eight or nine old ones around my cabin this summer. I hear they can live a really long time, and year after year they will travel back to the same den they were born in to have their babies. Humans rarely get bitten by snakes around here, but if you're not careful it can happen. Most of the time it is family pets that get bitten.

The newest house on the mountain belongs to a musician by the name of Samuel Fisher. He purchased twenty-five acres of land way up past Stash's place and the entrance to Why Worry. I hear from several people that he's a famous and eccentric fellow. He is the lead singer of the old rock group called the "Fisher Band." I haven't heard his music, but I guess he's recorded a few good albums. I've lost touch over the last several years without electricity. I don't see much television, and hear very little radio. All they play on my truck radio is country music, so I'm embarrassed to say that I don't know much about what's popular these days.

Peter says his band is pretty well known. Iris says, "he's single, ain't got no kids, and probably close to your age. What in the heck are you waitin' for chickipoo? You won't find no man if you don't start lookin'." I guess that's supposed to be some kind of hint. "Iris, he sure ain't no mountain man! I bet his hands are soft." Peter even joins in with a good laugh. The late sixties and seventies have ushered in a completely new culture of hard rock and roll, so I can't wait to hear him. I have seen him only on the road, in passing, when he's in town. I have to admit he sure picked a great place to come home to after all the time he spends on the road. So far no one else has started any new bulldozing or construction, but who knows what will happen next? Iris and Peter met up with the lady who is gonna build a new house closest to them. Her name is Margaret Beck. Iris has taken a shine to her, and enjoys her company when she comes up from Florida to meet with local contractors. She's building a log cabin too, and her's will be the next house started on the mountain. For now all is quiet again, and the rattlers have retreated back to their dens.

CHAPTER THREE

Fall is here faster than any of us are prepared for. The hardwoods are already heading into full color. The trees are stunning this year, and the leaf-lookers can't be more pleased. Halloween is just about here, and just that fast winter is already around the corner. The Farmer's Almanac, Riley, Stash, and the wooly worms all predict a brutally cold winter this year. The Great Smoky Mountain Appalachian way of life make Franklin very much a tourist town, and people come from all over to enjoy the culture. The Georgia highway dissects Macon County from south to north and is a main entrance point for many travelers coming up from the Deep South.

Thousands of people visit or pass through our small town every day. The mountains are full of precious stones, and gem mining is very popular. Franklin has been coined "the gem capital." The mountains are rich with minerals and a variety of gemstones. Rubies are most prevalent. There are stories of large gemstones mined from these hills worth millions. Tiffany's mined my property for emeralds and amethyst years ago. When I bought the property I also bought the mineral rights. It isn't anything to look down on the ground and find small rubies or sapphires. Most of them are just broken chips, but every now and then you find a pretty good sized one. The trick is to know what you are looking at. They may be gems, but until they're cut they look just like regular ol' rocks. Riley works part time in the gem business during tourist season, and she can tell you anything and everything you could possibly ever want to know about the subject.

The fall leaf season is our biggest cash season of the year. Last year was a disappointing fall 'cause the leaves turned brown and fell off early. It really hurt the local economy, and I depend on my artwork sales to make a livin'. Spring and summer business was good for me this year, but I need a great fall to make the winter more comfortable. I have several new paintin's ready to display, and I am hopeful that people will spend lots of money this year.

Iris, Peter, and all the folks at Why Worry are busy gettin' ready for harvest. The rain can set in for days, but I don't care, this is hands down still my absolute favorite time of the year. There is something poetic and profound about autumn. Somehow I can be happy and sad at the same time. When the sky clears after days of rain and the sun finally does come out, well, it's hardly describable. The air is crisp and clean, and the sky is the bluest blue you have ever seen.

The October colors frame White Rock magnificently. There is always an endless list of chores in the fall, but preparing for winter is a joyful time. We all know how important it is to get everything done in earnest. Hard work now will definitely affect our comfort come this winter. Why Worry Produce and Crafts has really gained in popularity with the tourists and local grocers this year. The collective farm is also starting to give the larger farms a real run for their money. This season was Why Worry's most profitable spring and summer ever, and we all hope and pray the fall crop will be as generous. The hippies, artist, musicians, and tree huggers will let their hair down in a monumental celebration of their bounty. I am sure this year's grand party will be the best one ever.

High spirits are palpable throughout the gap. We are all grateful and blessed. Luke and Anna are doing great, and beautiful little Miss Paisley is growin' like a weed. They're a striking family, and I feel sure that Paisley will not be an only child for very long. Stash is still working on his rustic cabin, and it is gonna be fabulous. He couldn't be more appreciative, and is working hard to make his buddy Scott proud.

We have finally met the people who bought the two hundred acres of land. Their names are James and Sylvia Graham. They're a young couple from Atlanta, Georgia. Mr. Graham is some kind of inventor. He's invented somethin' to do with "computers."

I'm not for sure what a computer is, but it must be something really important. It seems really complicated to me, but suffice it to say they made a big ol' truckload of money at a young age. The most important piece of information we all want to know is whether they have plans to split the property up and sell it off for a profit, or will they build and live on the land.

The thought of anyone splitting up this land makes me sick to my stomach. If I had the money I would by the whole gosh darn mountain. I'm getting worked up thinking about it, and I tell myself to calm down. "Don't get all wigged out before you even know what is going on." I have to put my trust in the Lord that he has a good plan for all of us that live here.

Here comes trouble driving up my road. "Riley, what are you up to? I can't take any worse news, so please don't even go there. I'm just gettin used to Mr. Fisher livin on the mountain."

The news may actually be good judging by the look on her face. You can't always tell with her? "Okay, Riley, lay it on me, now what's goin' on around here?"

Riley looks serious at first and then can't stand it any longer. She finally breaks out laughing.

"Riley Stone, you never could keep a straight face!" It fells like a ton of worry falling off the back of my neck and shoulders after hearing her whole story. "You're kiddin me? The news is not only good, but it's great. I could kiss you, Riley Stone, but I'll settle for a great big hug!"

Riley is not a touchy-feely kind of person. Her daddy didn't show her much affection growing up. Every now and then I catch her off guard and can get a kiss and hug in. The girl says that she hates it, but I don't care.

The long and short of the story is Sylvia Graham has a passion for Tennessee Walking horses. Around here we just call 'em "Tennessee Walkers," and turns out that she owns several prizewinners. She has always dreamed of owning and operating a breeding ranch, and the land is perfect for her new business adventure. The best news is the ranch will be their permanent residence. They have already decided on a name for the mountain ranch. It will be called Tessentee Stables. Tessentee is the name of the main road that connects White Rock Mountain and Hickory Gap to the outside world. James and Sylvia are like swanky tree huggers and have no intention to develop the land. The information couldn't be better, and I know Stash will be overjoyed.

The large swath of land they purchased is surrounded by the perfection and beauty of the Great Smoky Mountains. It is located on acres and acres of pristine pastures, mountain lakes, and the finest mountain land anywhere in this county. The breeding ranch promises to be impressive when it's finished. What I have seen so far is breathtakingly beautiful. By far the prettiest ranch I've ever seen. The whole place is shaping up to be out of this world.

Several more acres are sold in Hickory Gap not long after the Grahams move in. The allure of our private paradise is slowly attracting a trickle of folks. We see our charmed lives change before our very eyes, and White Rock Mountain is revealed to the outside world. We cannot stop the progress, so our only option is to embrace it. There is still plenty of breathing space for all of us to live remotely and peacefully. Thankfully, so far no one has a problem with Why Worry.

Stash and I both need to go to town, so we plan to make a day of it. I try to go off the mountain at least once a month. I gather every necessity I may need, including drinking water and containers of gas. You just never know. These days it seems like the whole country is falling apart, and everything is a crisis! I planned to meet him down on Hickory Gap road in the morning. Hickory Gap is an old logging gap. I guess at one time you could get over to Scaly Mountain through the gap, on a series of old loggin' trails. The Scaly Mountain community is a small outpost town accessible now to traffic going up to Highlands, North Carolina. Hickory gap to Scaly Mountain is no longer easily passable, but the old loggin' road still exists somewhere under all the years of forest decay.

Riley and I are enjoying the sunset out on the front porch. The coffee tastes good, and the view is grand. There is a chill in the air, but I won't need any heat tonight. "Ya' know Sonny this is the life. Yep, yep, we sure do live in God's country." I'm sipping my coffee and pondering things. "Sure enough. Nebraska seems like a long time ago." It's getting late, so Riley decides to crash on the sofa, and she is always welcome company. Her dad knows that if she doesn't call him she's on the mountain somewhere.

Johnny Stone can take care of himself, but he's an old man these days. Sometimes he doesn't have the common sense to stop, and there is all kinds of mischief for him to get into at home. I tell Riley, "If he ever stops and sits down, it will be the end of him."

She just laughs and nods her head in agreement. "You are right about that, Sonny Branch. You are right about that!"

The gap is foggy this morning, but I see Stash sauntering down the road. I holler at him. "Come on, old man, you're burnin' daylight!"

He smiles, heads for the truck, and jumps in next to me. I packed a small cooler of soda pop for the road trip and offer him one. Then we head to town. Stash looks good this morning. "Well, Stash, you sure clean up well." Smiling, he lights up a joint, takes a big drag off of it, and like always politely offers it to me.

He knows I don't smoke, but I guess it's the respectful thing to do. If I ever did smoke with him, he would probably freak out. I know a lot people that smoke pot, but Stash is the only one I will allow to smoke it in my truck. The way I see it, Daniel Calabash fought for this country. He says it helps him get through life. Who am I to judge?

I prefer him stoned and mellow rather than drunk and foul-mouthed. He is talkative, funny, and engaging when he smokes his marijuana. He's gets just plain mean when he drinks. Stash can solve all the problems of the world when he's high, and I love that side of him. It's positive and patriotic. He is a good-looking guy, and when you spend time with him, it's easy to see why he has plenty of girlfriends. And he sure does love to talk politics. Whenever Peter and he are together, they always go round and round.

It happens to be my least favorite topic. It's a known fact people kill each other all the time over politics. I listen politely, render an occasional opinion, but try to change the conversation every chance I get.

We just pass the entrance to the Bartram trail heading down Tessentee road. The well-known trail leads hard-core enthusiasts to the top of White Rock Mountain. The mountain has a fantastic flat rock face, and mountain climbers come from all parts for the challenge. Right off my back porch, large groups of climbing clubs can be seen through binoculars repelling and traversing the bald. There aren't any signs along the road that indicate to the public that the Bartram trail is even here. Only avid hikers and climbers know where the entrance to the trail is located. Occasionally we'll see vehicles sitting abandoned for hours and sometimes days at a time. Those of us that travel this road most don't pay it much attention.

Just passed the trail entrance, two men standing on the side of the road come into view. "Hey Stash, check it out. There's two dudes waiving us down." They are standing next to an old pickup truck. Both men anxiously begin waving their arms to get our attention. "Yeah I see 'em. Let's check it out." We pull in behind the truck, and they come walking toward us.

Stash jumps out the door first. "Hey, what's up?"

The older of the two guys has a gruff voice. "My name is Hank Greene." I'm guessing he's probably in his early fifties. The sun can definitely age a person, and you can tell he's worked outdoors for years. He gestures to his friend. "This here's Jude Turner."

Jude looks to be my age. He tips his hat and sheepishly nods his head, acknowledging me. With a soft-spoken voice replies, "Ma'am." Light blue eyes, dimples when he smiles, and a head of coal black hair is all I can make out under his cowboy hat. He is definitely very tall and well built.

Stash pokes me in the side. "Sonny, the two men are obviously burning up and dog-tired."

Hank speaks up. "We're not from around here. We just got hired on at the Graham place. We're the new ranch hands. We were headed that way, and my ol' truck tore up. Do you know how much further up the road the Tessentee stables are?"

Stash looks at me, and without any hesitation we both agree to take them to the ranch. "Jump in the truck, and we'll take you there. Your old truck almost made it. It's up ahead just a few miles. My name is Sonny Branch, and this is Daniel Calabash."

He nods civilly and tells the two men to call him Stash.

They accept our invitation for the ride and don't waste any time jumping into the back of the truck. I told Mr. Greene to leave his truck on the roadside. "You can fetch it later. No one will bother it." I give them both a cold soda out of the cooler. Stash and I hop into the front seat and can't help looking at each other with excited curiosity.

Stash is the first one to speak. "Well, they seem like all right guys."

I lean over and whisper in his ear. "I'm not sure if you're serious or just being a smart ass this morning,

49

Daniel Calabash." I punch him in his arm, and he sniggers under his breath. We head back toward the mountain. I have to admit Jude caught my eye. "Jude seems to be a pretty nice guy? Not bad lookin' either. Yep, not to shabby." He smacks my arm. "I've never seen you so flustered over some dude?"

We arrive at the main entrance of Tessentee stables. I notice in my rearview mirror that both men are collecting their belongings and getting ready to jump out when we stop. Hank and Jude both thank us politely for the ride and begin their walk to the main house. They both hold up their arms and wave good-by once they go through the big black wrought iron gate. I honk in response and head up the gap home.

The day is still young, but Stash decides to reschedule our trip to town. I drop him back off at his place. Stash notices that I've been grinnin' like an ol' cheshire cat. "Hey girl thanks for the interesting morning. Maybe we can hit town later in the week." "You betcha buddy. Life is never boring when you're around. I probably wouldn't have stopped to pick those fellers up if you weren't with me!" On the ride home I can't help but think the day hasn't been a total waste of time. I did get to meet Jude Turner, and he is definitely a very interesting guy.

Riley's already left, to who knows where, when I get home. I feel lazy today. There's a chill in the cabin, but the sun will warm the house soon. I don't want to fool with the woodstove, so I wrap myself in a blanket and go sit on the front porch. The sun is warm on my face, and I find myself drifting off to sleep in the rocking chair. I wake up with a crick in my neck after about an hour. The rest of the day wasn't a total washout after I woke up from a great nap. I managed to get a lot of chores done.

The next morning I am startled wide awake by the sensation of somebody watching me sleep. I look over, and someone's sitting in the chair next to my bed. I gasp and then realize who it is. "Riley Stone, you scared the crap out of me!"

Riley laughs. "I could have been anyone. You do remember that strangers are moving to White Rock?"

I can't help but laugh. "I must admit that guy Samuel Fisher seems kinda odd. Why are you here anyway?"

"I'm going to the feed and seed. Do you wanna go with?"

Still gettin' over bein' startled out of my sleep. I reply in a slightly annoyed voice. "All right, all right, let me get dressed and wake up a little bit. What time is it?"

Riley in her usual perky voice answers. "It's nine o'clock. Now hurry and get dressed."

I cannot wait to tell Riley about Jude. I start chattering like a crazy woman before we even get out the front door. I'm not sure I ever took a breath, and before I know it we're already at Baxter's feed and seed. I think Riley is in a state of shock. She hasn't been able to get a word in edgewise. "Riley, I can't remember the last time that I've had feelings stir over a man. It's been a really, really long time. Not just any man, but a total stranger."

The new wood splitters draw my attention away from Riley once we get out of the truck. I'm looking at price tags, turn around, and literally run into Jude

Turner. He's standing right behind me. "Jude, wow, I didn't expect to see you again so soon. How did things go at the ranch yesterday? Are you and Hank getting settled in?" I'm not sure if he even remembers me, but I have definitely been thinking about him.

Riley spots us from a mile away. I am talking to an unknown man that looks very much like my description of the now infamous Jude Turner. She falls all over herself running over to join us and butts into the conversation. "Hi, I'm Riley. Best friend of Sonny Branch!" Then she starts to sing the song "Hey, Jude" by the Beatles, and I am completely and totally mortified. Riley Stone is a dead woman, and I have plenty of places to hide her body.

"Jude Turner, this is Riley Stone, my good friend." I turn to Riley, squint my eyes, and before I can finish a sentence she interrupts me again.

"I know, I know, you're Jude, the new ranch hand. I've already heard all about you." Riley follows up with an eager laugh, and I follow her laugh with a smack to her arm.

Jude greeted us both respectfully, but I can tell there is something weighing on his mind. I quickly speak up before Riley has the chance to say anything else. "Jude, you look worried. What's wrong?"

His voice is full of concern. "One of the mares is foaling. The veterinarian hired by the Grahams hasn't gotten to the ranch yet. I need to get some supplies before the local vet gets out to help with the birth."

Riley in all of her glory offers my help. "Sonny can help you. She's delivered tons of human babies!"

I look at her and grit my teeth. "I'm sure Mr. Turner doesn't need my help." I want to make plain my anger with her, but she knows that I will hold back in front of Jude. This is her way to get all kinda stuff stirred up, and she loves every minute of it.

Jude takes us both by surprise. "I'll take all the help I can get! You guys can follow me back to the barn. Oh, and by the way, Sonny, I would love to hear about those babies one day. You have my curiosity piqued."

Riley immediately speaks for both of us. "Sure, we'll follow you back to the ranch." Jude quickly places several bales of straw into the bed of his pickup truck. "The ranch hasn't produced any straw or hay yet, and I need to make sure there is plenty of clean bedding."

Caravan style we head toward the stables. I look at Riley. "Well, well, our day is promising to be quite exciting. Much better than I was expecting, but be sure I am still mad at you."

Riley grins at me. "Well, well, indeed. You seem to be quite smitten with this Jude Turner guy."

I dismiss the comment and continue to stare out the window, thinking to myself. Maybe I am. Maybe I am, I can't ever stay angry at that woman, and she knows it. When we arrive at the barn, Jude swiftly prepares the birthing stall. They have special rooms in the barn set up just for foaling. This will be the very first birth at Tennessee stables.

Jude's attention to the horse is nothing short of brilliant. He's confident, at ease, and his voice is cool and calm. The first thing he does is to make sure the mare stands and walks. He's hoping to prolong the impending birth. Jude looks down at his watch and then at me. "The vet should be here any minute."

Riley and I watch everything quietly from a short distance away. We whisper to each other about how absolutely magnificent this place is.

Riley says, "This is the cleanest barn I've ever seen. I swear you could eat off the floor." There are at least twenty horse stalls, and I guess that probably half of them hold fine looking Walker's.

"I'll let the mare do her own thing," Jude says. "We're only here in case of an emergency."

I am so excited, and watching Jude handle the mare is really impressive. I cannot believe this is all happening. What an experience.

Hank Greene walks into the barn with Stash. "Is she ready, Jude?" Jude looks at Hank with a slight irritation, but he replies civilly. "Yep, it won't be much longer." It appears that Hank Greene and Stash have something in common; they're both drunk as skunks.

I whisper to Riley. "Dang, I hate that!" Stash is a good man, but he has a serious drinking problem. He always has ever since I've known him.

Stash speaks to me in a slur. "Hey, Sonny. I didn't know you were gonna be here. I heard about the foal and thought I'd come along with Hunter to watch." Riley and I aren't rude, but he knows how we both feel about his drinking.

It feels like an eternity, but the veterinarian finally arrives. She has everything they will need for the birth. Jude introduces her to everyone. "This is Dr. Christina St. Mark." She politely nods at Stash, Riley, and me. She makes her way over to where the visibly nervous mare is standing. She acknowledges Hank Greene respectfully, but in his current drunken condition she firmly requests that he stand out of the way. She suggests that maybe he move over to the railings with the rest of us and watch. He moves begrudgingly and stands next to Stash.

Riley speaks softly in my ear. "She looks like she comes from money. "I quietly respond. "Will you hush, Riley? She's gonna hear you talking about her."

Dr. St. Mark slowly and calmly approaches the horse to assist Jude in lying her down. In a thick French accent, she tells Jude her observation. "The water sac is full to bursting." She asks him to hand her some kind of sterile instrument that looks like a big ol' crochet hook. She uses it to poke a hole into the bulging bag. Amniotic fluid gushes out and soaks both Dr. St. Mark and Jude.

I watch Jude interacting with the doctor. He is at least six-foot five, and not a thin man, just a big man. I bet he is very muscular under all that denim and flannel. His eyes are serious and captivated as he listens intently to Dr. St. Mark. You can tell he has a long history of working outside. His tan gives him away. I notice Riley is checking him out. I jab her in the side with my elbow and end any ideas she may have real quick. She grabs her side and laughs. "Damn, Sonny! That hurt!"

We can hear Dr. St. Mark explain in simple terms to Jude what she thinks is about to happen. This will be the first time she has worked with him, and I'm sure she wants to make sure he is competent in what he's doing. Her French accent is enthralling. I love listening to the information and pay attention intently. "In a normal birth the front hooves would come first. One slightly ahead of the other, just out to about their knees. After closer examination I've determined this delivery will be breach." She speaks with self-confidence and clarity. "The hocks are coming after the hooves, and I can see the tail!" There is a dead quiet in the room. Jude assures her that he is prepared and ready to help.

Riley leans into me. "This ain't his first rodeo!"

I giggle back. It didn't take long for the foal to be born once the horse's water broke. Christina and Jude successfully pull the foal through the birth canal assisting the mare in the birth. A round of polite applause breaks out around the stall. I look over, and Hank and Daniel are missing. Who knows where?

Mom and baby take a much-needed rest. It is a lovely and awesome sight to observe. Jude looks over at me, and his dimples accent a prideful face. "This is the life, Sonny Branch!"

I return the smile. "I totally agree, Jude Turner."

Dr. St. Mark finishes with the mare while Jude carefully dips the foal's cord in iodine to prevent any infection. Riley and I decide to get out of the way now that all the excitement is dying down. We take one quick last look at the foal and mama before Jude walks us out to the truck. I wave goodbye to Dr. St. Mark as we head out the door. She graciously returns the gesture. Stash and Hank are busy in the tack room, and I didn't get a chance to say goodbye to either of them.

Jude opens the truck door for me and kindly thanks both of us for coming. Once we are home, Riley and I rehash the day's events over a glass of wine.

"Thanks, Riley! That's all I can say!"

She nods her head. "Sonny, I don't know what was more beautiful, the foal or Jude?"

I just look at her. "Ha, ha, I'm more interested in Stash and Hank. Now that's a pair!"

Riley leans back in the sofa. "Who cares? I wanna talk about today."

I sigh. "Riley Stone, you beat all I've ever seen!"

Our first day of light snow is here. The air is fresh and invigorating. I am chopping kindling when I notice Samuel Fisher walking up my drive. I've only seen him in passing, and haven't actually talked to him yet, so I'm intrigued. He saunters over to where I'm standing. He is clearly struggling for a breath, and speaks to me in a careful and measured voice. "Sonny, we haven't met yet. My name is Sam Fisher. I'd love to talk. Do you have the time?"

I'm hesitant at first, but I am interested to meet him. I have had some seedy characters come to my door in the past, but he looks pretty darn harmless. "Mr. Fisher, what can I help you with?"

He responds. "Please call me Fish. That's what I've been called my whole life."

I politely nod. Everybody these days has a nickname of some kind. What's up with that? He continues his conversation. "I haven't had a chance to stop by yet. I hope this isn't a bad time?"

I prop my ax on the chopping stump. "No, not at all, this is a fine time." I motion him to walk with me up the steps and take a seat on the front porch.

I have been curious about this guy ever since he moved to the mountain, and his presence now gives me the chance to "yak" with him. Fish looks like he is maybe the same age as I am. He is not a big man, has long dirty blonde hair, and a mustache. He seems to be a nice enough guy, but definitely not my type like Iris was hinting at. He doesn't look much like a mountain man, and I doubt he can chop wood. The hike from his house to mine is challenging for even the fittest hikers.

When he reaches the top of the stairs, you can tell he is out of breath. He looks around the porch and sits in the closest chair he can find. It only takes a few min-utes before he is able to catch his breath. "That is one heck of a walk!"

I smile. "How far is it from your place?"

Fish laughs at the question. "Obviously the hike is too far for me! I'm clearly out of shape."

We both snigger out loud. I have conceded to myself that he is on the mountain to stay, so I offer him something to drink and make polite conversation. "Ah, don't worry Fish, we'll make a mountain man out of you yet." He doesn't look so convinced, and I laugh.

Samuel Fisher built a stunning log home, and for the first time there is electricity going through the gap. There have been few chances or time to really get to know much about him. I hand him a drink out of the cooler. "Sorry, Fish, all I have is soda pop. Stash drank my last beer." He takes a glance around. "That's a beautiful view of White Rock."

"So what brings you to our neck of the woods, Mr. Fisher?" There is an uncomfortable moment as he continues to look around. "Oh, I mean Fish." I laugh, and he laughs.

The silence is broken, and our chitchat is really easy and pleasant. He seems perfectly witty and harmless. He tells me that he's on the road a lot. "I came in a few days ago and thought I'd take the chance you would be here."

I love all of his stories about the band life, groupies, and all the journeys that he has taken in his life. I often forget there is a whole other world off this mountain. He pulls out a joint from his front pocket and lights it. He takes a big puff off it and then hands it to me.

I was not surprised or offended. "Fish, you're welcome to smoke it, but I don't partake. I think there are times I definitely could use it."

We both laugh it off. He takes a couple of hits off his joint, snubs it out, and places it back in his front pocket. Fish tells me a little bit about growing up in Atlanta, and about his family. We both enjoy several more minutes of talking until suddenly there is a long pause. We both forgot what we are talking about.

"Fish, it must notta been important."

He stands up to leave. "Well, I thought I'd come by and share a buzz with you. I figured you smoked." He suggests that the next time he's in town we should all get together. "We can have a rockin' cookout at my place. I'd love for you to check it out. You'll really dig it."

I smile, semi-agree, and point at my pile of wood. "I have to get this wood chopped before the first big snow comes." He's a pretty nice guy, and easy to talk to. He throws up two fingers. "OK, I'll catch up with you, peace out!" I watch him meander down the hill until he's out of sight.

The mountain is slowly filling in with a patchwork of people. You can hear the distant sounds of hammers and saws, and Hickory Gap road actually has traffic on it. The other newest member of Hickory Gap and White Rock is Margaret Beck. She finally moved into her new log home, and Iris can't be happier. I have only seen her a few times, and to me she doesn't seem at all friendly. She is an older woman and looks to have a permanently disapproving expression on her face. She and Fish have also become good friends, and through him, I am learning more about her. I have yet to speak to the woman, and I shouldn't jump to conclusions about her. I had reservations about Fish when he first moved here, and I admit that he's turned out to be a pretty good feller. Odd and curious, but truly a nice guy.

Now that more people have moved to the gap, we get postal service. We all have an official mailbox now just a short piece down Hickory Gap road. I walk to get the mail every day, and I must confess, its [word choice?] pretty friggin' cool to have my own address and mailbox. I don't get much in it yet, but when I do, it's excitin'.

I'm standing near the short row of mailboxes, and a red vehicle is coming up the road. I realize that it's Margaret Beck. She eases her car toward me with caution, and to my surprise stops the vehicle next to where I stand. Assuming she wants to get her mail, I politely move out of her way. She has a horrible look on her face and rolls down the window. "Do you have any business on this road?" she asks.

I was incensed at first, but soon realize that she is just a spindly and frail woman who doesn't look to be in real good health. Her coloring is poor, and she looks very underweight. I tell her who I am. "I live up at the first left around the curve; my name is Sonny Branch."

The woman is in a surly mood and gestures me out of her way. Margaret collects her mail and continues up the gap, and all I can do is shake my head. "It's definitely gettin' interestin' round here."

Once she drives off and I stand quietly and open my mail. Jude shows up suddenly. "Hey, Sonny, how are you today?"

Startled but pleased, I eagerly reply. "Hi, Jude! How's the mare and new foal?" He smiles, and his dimples distract me. I coyly return the gesture.

"Sonny, they're doing really great. Thanks for all your help the other day." I graciously accept his nicety. "You're welcome, Jude."

He grins again. "Maybe we can do it again some time? Better yet, Sonny, I still want to hear about all the babies you have delivered."

We both laugh. "I would love that, Jude."

I excuse myself after an awkward pause, and with my mail in hand, I continue back up the mountain. I feel his eyes on me as I walk away. I turn around to see if he is watching me walk back up the road. He is definitely staring. I wave and continue up the mountain. I am no doubt beginning to like at least one of my new neighbors! He is downright good looking! My walk home has been a good one. I reach the cabin in record time and realize that I have been grinning all the way back up the road. I think to myself, "Sonny Branch, you are a little bit smitten."

CHAPTER FOUR

Thanksgiving is today, and we have an established tradition on White Rock Mountain. Everyone on the mountain joins Iris and Peter at Why Worry. I have not had an opportunity to hang out with Fish much, and I will get to officially meet ol' grouchy Margaret Beck. This will be the perfect time to get to know more about them both. Peter smoked a turkey outside in a contraption that he made from an old barrel, and several folks showed up with goodies in hand. Anna, Luke, and Paisley are here, and the baby looks so healthy. I scoop Paisley up in my arms, and we ease over to talk to Margaret.

Margaret welcomes our distraction, and she loves babies. After several minutes of just plain gabbing, she says, "Sonny, I retired from the telephone company down in Florida." She retired with a pretty good pension and moved here. Most retired people go to Florida. Not many move to one of the most remote areas they can find. "Far out Margaret! You picked a beautiful place to retire. These mountains can be difficult, but there ain't no place like home."

During dinner Margaret doesn't go into much detail, but she does mention that her health isn't good. She has some kind of an incurable persistent disease. It was some long name, but I take her at her word. She is very tall, well over six foot, and is super crazy skinny. I find out that she is only in her late fifties, not the late sixties or seventies that I first thought. Hardness exists in the creases engraved on her face, and I have a feeling that life wasn't always so good to Margaret Beck. I hope and pray that living here will bring her joy. Help her find the peace that she obviously and desperately seeks.

The more I listen, I get a peculiar feeling from her. She seems overly kind and attentive to Iris. It's almost out of the ordinary or over the top. I can't wrap my mind around it. To Peter and me, there is curtness in her action and tone of voice. Needless to say, I don't think she is one of my biggest fans. Stash is here and already pretty inebriated. Fish and Peter sit off in the corner discussing all of the current events.

Riley didn't come this year. She's home with her family today. Jude and Hank were invited to join us, and may still make an appearance later this evenin'. I surely hope so. They were invited to James and Sylvia Grahams home for dinner to mark their first Thanksgiving at the ranch. Iris has a good turn out for dinner this year. Everyone is leaving happy and stuffed. It is so nice to see everyone from Why Worry. The weather couldn't be more perfect, and there is an unexplainable calm today. "Iris honey, dinner was so tasty, but it's nap time, I'm gonna head to the house." The last few remaining folks say their goodbye's. I turn to wave. "Catch ya'll later!"

Thanksgiving has come and gone, and now Christmas is right around the corner. The mountain is brimming with the holiday spirit, and even grouchy ol' Margaret Beck is in a good mood. She's pretty much a loner just like the rest of us, but she loves to get off the mountain every day. She stays pretty busy judging by how much she goes up and down the road. She waves at me now when we cross paths, but I haven't spoken to her since Thanksgiving dinner.

Margaret is an odd and curious somebody. I can't help think she has secrets, and she's hiding from something or someone. There is more to her than she is telling, and no one else seems to notice it but me. I often wonder, "Who are you really, Margaret Beck?" Maybe she's a wanted criminal.

Iris thinks I'm being silly, so I purposefully discount my own feelings to her. "Crap youngin', we all have secrets."

This winter is Margaret and Fish's first full winter living on the mountain, and they are cautiously enthusiastic. I try to stop in and see Margaret when I can. She's tough to figure out, but we enjoy each other's company. I feel bad for all the awful things I said and thought. Heck, she ain't to bad at all. I can see why Iris digs her so much. We're sitting on her front porch, and I can't help but laugh talkin' about it. "Ah, Margaret, you're a tuff ol' broad!"

She actually laughs out loud for the first time that I can remember. "Sonny Branch, stop making me laugh!

I'm gonna pee my pants!" It is heartwarming to see a smile on her face. She does kinda seem like the motherly type, and she is really diggin' living on the mountain.

Margaret and Fish have also become close friends over the summer. Their personalities could not be more at odds, but when he's in town they both love to watch sporting events together on television. She loves to cook for him, and I'm sure he loves it back. They love Hickory Gap and White Rock Mountain just as much as the rest of us. The weather is going to change here over the coming days, and we all are soaking in the last bit of sunshine.

The recent days are the coldest I've seen since living in North Carolina. We are experiencing snow, record low temperatures, and wind chills. The sun is out but not melting the snow that remains on the ground and roads.

Riley could fill the pages of a book with the little quips she has learned growin' up, and this one always seems to be true. "When snow lies on the ground, it's waiting for another one." Hickory Gap is getting early snowstorms, one after the other, already this year. It appears that Stash, Riley, the almanac, and of course the wooly worm were accurate in their prior predictions. The snow earlier this week has already rendered Hickory Gap Road impassable to any type of vehicle. This new snow piles up on top the old snow and makes gettin' anywhere worse. The best four-wheel drive vehicle can't make it past my cabin.

The Grahams probably can't get out either. I imagine Jude and Hank have their hands full with the ranch.

I have not seen anyone in days, not even Riley. I bet she and Johnny are snowed in too. My hand held radio barely picks up Franklin's a.m. station, so I am somewhat keeping up with the weather, news, and the outside world.

The silence is becoming deafening after a week of bein' snowed in. The days pass slowly, and the stillness is nerve-racking. I know how to survive the winter weather, but after eight days I'm feelin' a deep sense of isolation. Painting usually fills my days, writin' makes my nights more bearable, but not even work can fill my days any longer. I pray that everyone on the mountain is out of harm's way and warm.

A sudden hard knock on the door is a jolt from out of the blue. I certainly didn't expect it, and I didn't hear anyone come up the road. I look out the window to see who it is, and to my surprise it's Peter.

I scurry to open the door. "How did ya' get here? I didn't hear you come up, and what in God's name are you doing out in this weather, Peter Benjamin? Is everyone all right?" I ask to take his coat, but he declines my offer.

He immediately walks over to the woodstove. Pulls off his hat and gloves and rubs his hands together over the heat. Fish and Margaret both have phone service, so when there's an emergency the news most likely comes from one of them. I doubt they have any telephone or electricity right now.

Peter catches his breath. "Sonny, Fish is concerned about Margaret Beck. He wasn't able to reach her by phone and went down to check on her. She's gone!"

"Peter, what do you mean she's gone?"

"Sonny, Fish is convinced something bad has happened to her." The temperatures are falling quickly, and the sun is setting. Margaret Beck is not in the best of health, and the news of her disappearance is alarming. "Sonny, we need everyone's help to look for her."

I quickly prepare the woodstove. It won't last all evening, but at least the cabin will be warm for a while longer. Peter tells me that several people are already at her place searching. My truck won't make it up to Margaret's, so I leave on the four-wheeler with him.

We head to Margaret's house. The road is slick, and the ride is rough. We are utterly flyin' in the snow. It takes all kinds of muscles just to keep myself on the four-wheeler. I notice Riley first when we arrive at Margaret's. "I thought you were at home, Riley."

She got stranded at Peter and Iris's when the last snowstorm hit and just stayed there. My attention to Riley doesn't last long, and I see Jude waving from a distance. Riley said he's been here for a while. That must mean Hank Greene is close behind.

We are searching every square inch of the mountain for any sign of Margaret, but no one has been able to find her. Flashlights and lanterns help navigate the rough terrain in the darkness. Fish is visibly upset. He was the first one to arrive at her house and fretfully recounts his story to me.

"Sonny, I found the garage door open. The driver side door of her car was open, her keys are in the ignition, and her purse is lying on the front seat undisturbed. There was no sign of Margaret. What could be so important that she would attempt to go anywhere in this weather?"He continues his story. "The basement door was left wide open, and it doesn't appear to be damaged by a break in. I walked through the house calling her name loudly, but there was no answer. I went through every room and looked in every closet, but I didn't find her. Sonny, I even looked over the bank next to her house, but I still couldn't find her!" Fish was able to get a phone line out from Margaret's and called the local police. The weather is a big obstacle for anyone to reach Margaret's house from town, but the police is sending someone out right away. The cops will put a four-wheeler in the back of their trucks when there's an emergency and will drive in as far as they can. If they run into an impassable situation along the way, they'll ride the four-wheelers to their final destination. Either way, the officers will be here as quickly as they can.

Stash was one of the first to arrive after Fish. Stash is a strong leader and quickly forms a strategy to look for her. The skills that Stash and Peter learned in the military will be invaluable to help us look for Margaret. Exposure to this bitter cold and snow will be deadly if Margaret is out there somewhere in it.

Hank is walking along with numerous folks from Why Worry. We don't let the weather stop our hunt, and everyone continues to frantically search. I can hear calls for Margaret all over the mountain. Fish is no longer able to continue and stands alone in the dark watching down the road for any glimpse of police and rescue.

Suddenly out of the woods and in the darkness we all hear. "I found her! I found her!" The declaration echoes through the holler, and I can hear the ramblings of everyone heading towards the voice of Hank Greene.

We all emerge from various points in the woods to the site of a large ravine nearby Margaret's house. Hank makes his way down the steep gorge to where he sees her lying. We all wait anxiously for the news, but sadly he confirms our worst nightmare. "She's gone!"

Sobs and gasps replace a cold silence. Our flashlights guide Hank's pathway back up the ravine. My flashlight moves over Margaret's frail, still body in the dark narrow valley. She is curled up in the fetal position. The thin sweater she is wearing was no match for these record low temperatures. It stuns me how fragile life can be, and I say a private prayer for her.

Fish and Iris knew her the best. She mollycoddled both of them all the time. My encounters with her were always cordial, but cold and aloof. My only hope is that she died rapidly. I wouldn't wish this horrible tragedy on anyone.

We all gather back at Margaret's house and wait for the police to arrive. Fish says their electricity has been out for days, but thank God the phone lines didn't go down. Jude, Riley, and I stand together in the dark waiting. I can hear murmurings from small groups of people in the shadows questioning how this could possibly happen. "How did she get down there?" "There is something not right." "Did someone kill her?"

I will never forget these hours of obscurity as long as I live. It's so real that it almost seems like a dream. We all hear Fish shout out. "I can see lights coming up the gap!" I hear a harmonious sigh of relief from everyone. "Finally the police have arrived!"

It has been two hours since we found Margaret. Dismayed with the news of her passing, a lot of folks from Why Worry have already gone home. Luke has been deathly sick but made an earlier appearance. Unfortunately, he had to leave before we found her. The red and blue lights of emergency vehicles now consume the darkness.

They slowly make their way up through the gap, and it is not long before the bright flashing lights engulf Margaret's entire home place. One of the officers comments that the road was really bad, but their trucks managed to get through. The cops follow Hank and Stash as they make their way over to the edge of the gorge and point down to where she is lying several feet below.

The younger officer volunteers to climb down the ravine first. The other cop and Hunter follow him down. Stash stays at the top so he can light their pathway. Hank guides them both to her exact location, and they reach her with relative ease. They talk for a few minutes and document the time of death for their records.

Hank tells them that he found her during the search. "I went down there, and she was dead. I could tell she was dead by looking at her. I didn't move or touch anything. She is lying there exactly like I found her."

The officers pat his shoulders with compassion, and they all head back up the embankment.

The officers discuss and debate the best way for Earl Young to bring her up from the bottom once they reach the top. I guess he'll go down into the ravine and carry her up once all the evidence is collected. Earl also works at the funeral home, and owns his own gravel hauling company. They won't move her body until a thorough investigation of the area is complete, and then the coroner's office will come to get her. The actual coroner is in Sylva, so they'll take her to the local hospital pending an autopsy.

I overhear the cops say to each other that this could take hours to wrap up, and it may be tomorrow before they can make it up here to pick up Margaret's body. It all depends on the weather and road conditions. Poor Margaret may end up lying down there till daylight. Riley is impatient and wants to get this wrapped up. She's tired, cold, and hungry. The thought of staying here all night with Margaret lying down in the ravine is freaking her out, but Jude and I are preparing to stay with Peter and Iris for the long haul if they need us.

The cops begin a brief address asking that no one else leave before they get a chance to talk to them. They're taking turns explaining what they would like us to do before going home. Fish asks the question that is on everyone's mind. "Do you think it was an accident, or was she murdered?"

"Jude, Riley, did you catch what Fish asked?" I found it a curious question considering he was here before anyone else. Maybe hours who knows? "Wow you guys for all we know he could have killed her? He's kinda peculiar." I look suspiciously toward Riley and Jude, and in return they just laugh at me. "Ha! Ha! Ya'll laugh at me if you want. Well, do we really know that much about him? He comes and goes all the time. Hey, you guys don't know him."

Riley can't help herself. "What about Hank Greene? He's a good suspect."

Jude looks at me and then at Riley. "He may be a washed up ranch hand and a drunk, but I don't think he's a killer." We are freezing, but we are geared up to stay for a while to wrap this up.

The young officer begins his questioning directed toward me and asks my name first. He goes on to inquire. "Ms. Branch, I need all the information you can recall about your neighbor today."

I briefly glance over at Jude before I respond to his question. "The weather has kept me inside for going on eight days, and I haven't seen anyone till today. Peter Benjamin showed up at my place earlier this evening. He told me what was going on, and that's the first I heard about Margaret's disappearance." My teeth are chattering from the cold and my nerves. I'm on edge, and they won't stop.

Trying to calm my anxiety, Jude instinctively puts his arms around me. The cop is satisfied with my information and gives me permission to go on home. The officer talks to Jude next, and after a brief exchange allows him to also leave.

Riley of course starts to talk nineteen to the dozen. "Officer, I'm Riley Stone." She takes a breath, smiles at him, and then at me. I wrinkle my forehead and fix my gaze on her eyes. I plead silently, "Please behave!"

Riley is my best friend, and she reads me like a book. She knows exactly what I am thinking when I look at her.

Jude interrupts the awkward moment. "Officer, is there anything else that Sonny or I can do for you tonight?" Jude gently squeezes my shoulders.

The police officer respectfully dismisses us both but continues his inquiry of Riley. I don't have my vehicle here, and I am possibly at her mercy for a ride home. Who knows how long that could be?

Jude notices me shivering and offers to drop me off at home on his way back down to the ranch. I am cold and stunned by the whole night, and my patience is wearing thin. I butt into Riley's conversation with the young officer. "Sorry to interrupt you. Riley, I'm going home, are you gonna crash at my place tonight?"

She winks and nods her head. "No thanks, Sonny. I don't know what I am going to do yet." She will probably stay with Iris and Peter. Who knows for sure? That girl is apt to stay anywhere.

There is one thing I have to say to Riley before I leave. I lean into her where she is standing, and whisper in her ear. "Riley Stone, you are a piece of work!"

She ignores my comment and continues to entertain the handsome young officer.

I turn my attention to Jude and graciously accept his offer for the ride home. "Thanks, Jude, I'd love a ride home." We walk down the road toward his parked four-wheeler. I can't make out what everyone else is saying as we pass by. They look up long enough to say goodbye. Then return their attention back to the officer and continue taking turns relaying their own versions of their story. My anticipation of the ride home is exciting. It has been a long time since I've felt this way about a man.

Fish volunteered to lock up Margaret's house after the investigation is over, and the police are gone. The police so far think it's probably an accident by all accounts. Somehow she wandered off in the woods, lost her balance, fell, and then probably froze to death. None of which explains why she was leaving in her car.

I notice that Hank Greene is pacing up and down the gravel drive waiting for his turn to speak with one of the officers. I can't blame him. It's freezing and been one hell of a night. We make eye contact. I smile, and nod my head at him in approval for a job well done. I'm glad he's the one who found Margaret. He and Stash have become drinking buddies, but other than that I don't know too much about him. Poor Margaret, I hate that she died all alone. No one deserves to die such a horrible death. These mountains can be brutal in the winter, but Margaret really loved them. I was really startin' to like her, and I think she was happy here. Jude shakes me out of my notions and helps me onto his four-wheeler. "Come on, Sonny, let me get you home."

CHAPTER FIVE

The ride home is extremely cold. We make our way through the gap, and the only noise I can hear is the loud thunderous engine of Jude's all-terrain vehicle. The sky is clear, and the stars are layers and layers deep. The snow is bright white under the full moon, and the wind is bitterly cold on my cheeks. I lay my face against Jude's back to protect it from windburn and hold onto his waist for stability. We make the final curve of the drive up to my cabin, and to my great surprise, I see smoke still coming out of the chimney. I expected to come home to a cold and dark house. To my relief there are obviously still some coals burning in the wood-stove, and thankfully it won't take long to get the house warmed back up.

Jude stops the four-wheeler next to the stairs going up my to my front porch. He hops off first, and without delay offers his assistance to help me. He holds onto my arm so I don't slip and fall walking up the front steps.

When we reach my front door I thank him for all that he has done to help out, and for the ride home.

His lips are on mine before I figure out what's happening. I'm surprised at first, but figure what the heck. It doesn't take me a split second to reciprocate his kiss. His hands are in my hair holding my face tight and close to his. His breath is heavy on my mouth, and his lips lie gently on my top of mine. I nestle my forehead on the bridge of his nose, and I am blessed beyond my wildest dreams. Is this really happening?

I tell myself more than once to just stop analyzing everything and enjoy it. I open my eyes slowly as I regain control of my wits. Jude's smile is reassuring and makes me feel better. He senses my awkwardness. "Sonny, I really am sorry about your friend's death. Will you be all right alone tonight?" He quickly realized what he may have suggested, and clumsily tries to explain his comment. "I didn't mean for me to stay here. That's not what I meant! I have a long day tomorrow at the stables, and it is getting late. May I see you again?"

I answer him in a whisper. "Yes, Jude Turner, I would like that."

He respectfully takes the keys from my hand and unlocks the front door for me. He takes his leave without delay once he is sure that I am safely inside. I can hear him walk back down the steps, and the engine starts. I watch him through the window until he rides out of my sight. I can still hear the four-wheeler for several more minutes as he makes his way down the gap and home to the ranch.

I actually have butterflies in my stomach for the first time in a long time. The only man I truly loved died when we were in our early twenties. We were engaged to be married, and our future was exciting. He died from an overdose of alcohol and drugs. He passed out on the bed after a late night of partying with buddies and strangled on his own vomit while he was sleeping. I spoke to him around midnight that night. I knew he was messed up, and he was begging me to come and see him. He lived clear across town, so I left out immediately. It was around two in the morning. Halfway there, my car broke down. I couldn't get it restarted. I walked to the closest payphone and called him for help. There was no answer. He died sometime between his plea for help and my plea for help. I always wonder if he would still be alive if I had made it there that night.

I moved to North Carolina from Nebraska shortly after he was buried. I had been to Franklin many years ago just passing through, but I remembered how much I loved the area. I needed a total change in attitude and surroundings. I quit my job, said good-bye to friends, and came here with no expectations whatsoever. His death changed the direction of my life, and I have not found anyone who has caught my interest ever since. I have been out on dates and enjoyed the friendship of a few men. I consider myself an attractive woman and stay in good shape for forty-two. I have not cut my hair in years, and so far it remains blonde with the exception of a few stray gray hairs trying to take over my whole head. What family I do have left are scattered. I don't consider myself a real feminine woman, but I can wear a pair of heels. The woodstove catches fire easily, and the cabin is warming up. What an evening. I say my prayers, and finally my mind starts to wind down. Where is Riley when I'm busting to talk to her? My last memory before falling asleep is of Jude's kiss.

Morning comes in a flash. There are several loud sharp knocks on the door, and the sudden noise jerks me out of a dead sleep. I shout out, "Yeah, yeah, I'm comin'. Don't get your bloomers in a wad!" I look out the window, and I see the sheriff along with two men in dark suits and overcoats. They're standing at my front door. They see me looking out the window and promptly display their badges through the glass. "We're detective's ma'am, and we need to talk to you about your neighbor Margaret Beck."

I tighten the belt on my tattered robe and shake out my hair, still half asleep. I open the door to invite everyone in and glance at the clock. It's only seven-thirty in the morning. Then the heartbreaking reality of the situation hits me. "Margaret Beck is dead."

They must have been working all night. I motion for everyone to sit down. My cabin is only seven hundred square feet, and seating can be a problem. The last remaining place to sit is on a homemade footstool that I made out of an ol' tree trunk. I carefully perch myself on it cause the dang thing toddles over real easy.

The sheriff starts the conversation first. "Miss Branch, how well do you know Hank Greene, Jude Turner, or Samuel Fisher?"

I know the look on my face is a blank, and it takes me a few minutes to absorb what he is asking. I hate being unnerved so early. I haven't had any coffee yet this morning, and my living room is full of men asking me questions. "Well, gentlemen, please forgive my empty stare, but I haven't had my coffee this mornin'." All three men politely smile, and patiently wait for my response to their question, so I guess coffee is out of the question for right now.

"I don't know much about Hank Greene other than he is not from around here. I think he is from Utah or Idaho. All I know is it's someplace out west. He hired on at Tessentee stables along with Jude Turner. Both men came together at the same time." My heart is sinking, and all I can think about is the kiss from last night.

The detective starts asking his questions. "Miss Branch, does Hank Greene go by any other name that you are aware of?"

I'm starting to shake. Not from the chill in the air or the intense need I have for a hot cup of coffee. I'm scared to death that this is not gonna have a good ending, but I answer civilly. "Yeah, Hank has mentioned that his nickname is Hunter, but I don't use it. Samuel goes by Fish, and Daniel Calabash goes by Stash. There, I think I covered all of 'em."

The next detective inquires about Jude. "What about Jude Turner? How much do you know about him?"

I clear my throat and squirm a bit on the stool. "I know Jude. I met him and Hank Greene the day they went to work for the Grahams, James and Sylvia. Their truck broke down on Tessentee. Daniel Calabash and I gave them a ride to the stables. Why you asking?"

The detective speaks calmly. "Ma'am, we aren't convinced that Margaret's death was an accident. In fact, Miss Branch, most of our information and evidence points to homicide."

I nod politely, but I can't believe what I am hearing. I admit to myself that it did cross my mind last night. I just thought I was being paranoid, but now I don't know what the heck to think. For god sakes are we harboring a murderer on the mountain? All the momentary thoughts are bombarding my brain, and causing that sinking feeling in my stomach. I have no time to respond to the detective before the sheriff asks me more questions. "What about Samuel Fisher? How much do you know about him?"

My mouth is suddenly very dry, and I can barely speak. "Gentlemen, will you please excuse me for just a minute? Can I get you all something to drink?" I stand slowly and deliberately. I have to catch my breath, and I'm in desperate need of something to drink. All three men stand as I go to the kitchen.

Once in the kitchen out of eyeshot of my company, I take a deep gulp of air and lean against the cabinets. "This can't be happening!" I grab the last can of pop out of the cooler and drink it straight down. It isn't cold, but that's all I have. I straighten my robe, take a deep breath, and walk calmly back into the living room.

"Sonny, tell us what you know about Samuel Fisher?"

I speak with candor and honesty. "I don't know Fish all that well. He travels a lot, and from what I hear his band is pretty famous." I pause and wait for more questions.

But instead all three men stand and thank me for my time. I'm still not sure what just happened, but I watch them as they drive down the hill. I let out a huge sigh of relief. They never did explain what is exactly going on. I am dying to find Riley and tell her all my news. Hopefully someone else around here knows what's going on.

I can't wait any longer, and I decide to head up to Why Worry on foot. Depending on the road, it may be easier to walk then risk getting my truck stuck some-where. The hike is actually pretty nice, and halfway there Riley meets me coming up the road in her truck. I was surprised to see her driving up the gap. She drove off the mountain last night after everyone left. She followed the coroner out with Margaret and spent the night at home. She hasn't been home in a few days and needed to check on Johnny.

Riley is relieved her daddy has been surviving just fine. "The roads are much better off the mountain. This place is a winter wonderland compared to town." She went up to my place and figured I was headed up to Why Worry when I wasn't home.

I tell her about Margaret's death becoming a mur-der investigation, and we decide to share the newest information together with Iris and Peter. I jump in the truck, and Riley heads up to Why Worry.

We decide to stop at Stash's place and get him on our way there.

I knock on his door. "Stash, you in there?" I figure that he is either passed out or gone.

After several bangs on the door and windows, we head up the gap without him. White Rock is snow-capped, and the ride up the gap is beautiful. The sun has made an appearance, and finally some of the snow is starting to melt off the dirt road. Christmas is just days away, and we have already had several inches of snow for the year. The wooly worms were jet black this year. The telltale sign that winter was gonna be a whopper. January and February will be interesting indeed if the snow keeps up.

All of a sudden White Rock is like a real life crime novel. I am still trying to process everything that has just transpired over the last twenty-four hours. I see Peter standing on the deck when we pull in the drive-way. I can tell immediately by the look on his face there is something horribly wrong.

"Peter, what's wrong?" I look around. "Where's Iris?"

He doesn't answer any of my questions. Instead he motions us to come up and then disappears back into the cabin. Riley and I walk up the steps together. Looking around, I can't help but think how much hard work and love they poured into building this place. I am still amazed every time I visit.

Iris is sitting on the couch in the living room when we come inside. She is distraught and clutching a necklace of some kind in her hands.

I glance at Peter and then at Iris. "Iris, what's wrong?"

Unable to speak, she hands me the necklace. Riley and I both look at it closely. It appears to be very old, maybe even an antique, some sort of locket. I carefully open it up, and inside it cradles the picture of a new-born baby. The baby in the picture cannot be more than a few hours old.

Riley asks Iris, "Who is it?"

In a distressed panic-stricken tone she whimpers, "It's me!"

Riley puts her arms around her and holds her tight. "Where did you get this? How can that be?"

Iris wails uncontrollably.

My heart is breaking for her. "Oh, Iris, I don't know what to say. Are you sure? How can you tell that it's you?"

Peter steps in to help Iris finish the story. "Iris was using the upstairs bathroom at Margaret's house and saw the antique locket lying in a crystal dish on the vanity. She wanted to see if there was a picture in it and opened it up. Iris recognized the baby and the blanket in the photo right away."

Iris breaks down crying again as Peter continues to recall the story. Riley and I are glued to our seats, waiting for Peter to finish the rest.

"Iris placed the locket in her pants pocket and ran home in a panic. I followed behind her. She immediately went to the bedroom closet and took out an old chest that she's had for years. The chest contains only a few items she managed to hold onto growing up. The very same handmade blanket that cradles the baby in the photo lies neatly folded under the memories of years gone by in that chest."

Iris is finally able to calm down some.

Riley and I are shocked at the news. "Margaret Beck was your mother?"

Iris stops sniffling long enough so we can understand what she is saying. "Why didn't she tell me, Sonny?" Her sobs are like a knife in your heart. They are gut wrenching. "Why did she keep her identity a big secret? Now she's dead, and I'll never know!"

Riley and I try to reassure her that we will help her find out all the answers. "We promise, Iris. Riley and I will do whatever it takes to help you get to the bottom of this."

A few minutes of silence pass, Iris leaves the room, and Peter looks at me. "You said there is new information you came to tell us?" he asks.

I almost forgot what happened earlier, and under the circumstances it is probably best that Iris left. "The local sheriff and two detectives came to my house this morning. They were asking about Hank, Fish, and Jude."

"What the heck? Are you kiddin' me?"

Riley breaks the news with great gusto. "Yeah, they told Sonny that Margaret's death wasn't an accident, it was murder. Jude, Hank, and Fish may be suspects."

Iris was walking into the living room and over hears the entire story.

Riley feels bad about her indelicacy explaining what happened. She forgot that Margaret could very well be Iris's mother. "I'm sorry, you guys, that was a terrible way to say it."

Peter looks at me. "Sonny, is that true?"

I nod. "Yes, they came by my place just a little while ago. Have they been up here yet?" I wanted to tell them about Jude's kiss, but I think it would sound pretty tacky under the circumstances. Jude may be the murderer of the mother you never knew, and by the way I'm falling in love him. I can't say anything about it right now, so with that I respectfully stand and say my good-byes.

"Riley, I'm heading back down the mountain. I don't want the cabin to get cold. Are you comin' with?" I squeeze Iris's hand. "Iris, we'll figure all this out, don't you worry. You ain't alone darlin'."

Riley decides to stay with Iris. I am pleased with her decision because I need some time to think. I don't mind the hike home. I hug Peter again on my way out the door. "Let me know if there's anything I can do."

The trip home doesn't take long, and I manage to make it to my sofa and collapse. The fire is out in the woodstove, but I don't give a crap. Can things possibly get any worse? I desperately miss Jude. I need reassurance and strength. I need his arms around me. There is no way he's involved in this. He is thoughtful and compassionate. The Jude Turner I know would never have anything to do with this awful tragedy. I haven't known him long, but the man I kissed last night told me everything I need to know about Jude Turner. He's not a criminal, and he is certainly not a killer.

CHAPTER SIX

A few days pass by, and I haven't heard anything from Jude. Hank and Stash have been missing since the night we found Margaret, and they are still missing. Fish is fuming. Iris is subdued but still in a state of shock. She is falling into a deep depression, and Peter is up in arms. It has been hard for me to wrap my head around the all the facts. "Margaret Beck is Iris Bell's mother! Oh my God!"

Riley told me the detectives came to Why Worry shortly after I left that day, and since then Iris can't stop crying. She said that Iris holds onto that baby blanket and locket like a wounded youngin'. The whole thing has everyone in a tailspin, and scratching our heads. What the heck happened to our mountain?

A soft knock on the kitchen window gets my attention, and for the first time in a long time I just can't bear any company right now. I sneak a quick look out of the curtains that cover a small side window in the kitchen. "Oh my God, it's Jude!"

He looks unkempt, nervous, and worried. He must be on foot because I didn't hear a vehicle come up. He sees the curtain move and starts calling my name. "Sonny, Sonny, I know that you are in there. I saw you lookin' out the window. Please, please, open the door. I need to see you!"

His pleading is heartfelt, and I am completely head over heels in love with this guy. I can't help myself and run to open the door.

"You are a sight for sore eyes, yes ma'am you are." He grabs me by both arms, kisses me passionately, and renders me speechless. "Somethin's goin' on that I need to tell you bout. I can't give you any answers right now, but I didn't do anything, and I'm workin' with the police. Promise that you believe me!"

I can tell he's in a hurry. "The Grahams are helping me, so please don't worry. I can't stay. I gotta get back to the ranch. I desperately needed to see you, and I couldn't stand it anymore. This should all be over soon." He is holding me tight in his arms.

"Jude, the sheriff and two detectives were here askin' about Hank Greene, Sam Fisher, and you! What's goin' on, Jude? Please tell me."

The detectives came to the ranch, and spoke with him that same day. "Sonny, I was told not to make contact with anyone till the murderer is in police custody. I'm not even supposed to be here, but I had to see you, pretty lady!"

Tears well up in my eyes immediately, and I beg him to tell me anything.

"Hank and Stash may have left together last night sometime and neither one have been around since. Sonny, I don't know where they're at. The police suspect Hank may be the killer. I've been asked to help bring him into custody, and the Grahams are in a full panic."

We hear a vehicle coming up the driveway, and I run to look out the living room window. I yell out to Jude. "It's okay. It's just Riley."

Jude doesn't answer me back, and I run back to the kitchen. He's already gone when I return, and the back door is left open. I stand in the doorway with tears in my eyes, but relief in my heart that he's at least safe and nearby. I am reassured by James and Sylvia Grahams' support. Jude Turner is a good guy, and I knew he couldn't be involved. I can at least take a deep breath now and wait for everything to finally come to an end.

I hear Riley coming through the front door. I close the back door and quickly swipe my eyes on the sleeve of my t-shirt. It's only a few seconds before she is walking into the kitchen. "Hey, you in the kitchen? Oh! There you are. Gosh, what's happenin' to everyone round here?" When Riley gets upset, her whimsical deep southern accent kicks into high gear, and I can't understand half of what she says.

I attempt to sit her down, but she is going full force like a bull in a china shop. "We need to talk. Please sit down." I finally start telling her about last night. I describe in detail how beautiful and peaceful the ride home was. Her eyes are the size of quarters. She knows that something good is comin'. I can see the anticipation growin' as I continue with my story. "He walked me to the door." Before I can even finish my sentence, she says, "What?" I tell her in a hushed voice. "We kissed, Riley! We kissed!"

I am not sure she is capable of speech at this moment judging from her reaction. I give her a second to respond. She jumps up from where she is sitting and grabs me great big. She doesn't realize her own strength, and I try to shake her off.

"Riley, stop it! You're gonna knock me down." I do not think it was going to be such a big deal, and I can't believe that she actually hugged me first.

"Sonny, it's about dang time!"

It is killing me not to tell her the new information about the case, but I choose not to tell her anything about Jude's brief visit. I need to figure out what in the heck is going on. Jude has really ignited a fire in my belly, and this whole nightmare needs to end. I cannot imagine what James and Sylvia Graham are thinking about all of this.

The results of Margaret's autopsy will take several weeks, but the county coroner has some preliminary information. The problem is there hasn't been anyone who has come forward to claim her body. The police haven't been able to find any next-of-kin. Margaret literally has no past. No one is able to find any information about her or where she came from down in Florida. That leaves Iris her only possible living relative, and I'm not sure she is ready to take on the responsibility alone. Margaret's death was heartbreaking, and no one should ever go unclaimed in life or death. Fish has already said he will request responsibility and give her a proper burial no matter what information comes out, and that news is comforting to everyone. Margaret owns her home and property outright. She must have access to cash, but there is no money trail for the police to follow. Her home place has been searched with a fine-tooth comb, and the entry doors have been sealed with yellow crime tape. No one is allowed in or out of the log cabin. Everything is hush, hush.

The story has made the front page of the town's paper as well as the Asheville nightly news. The local people are saddened and unnerved by the reports. No one has seen Stash since the night of Margaret's homicide. I hope he's with buddies down in Georgia. Hank is still on the lam, wanted for questioning of Margaret's murder. Fish has been cooperating extensively with the police, and from what Jude told me, he isn't a suspect. I feel sure that Fish will be cleared of any wrongdoing. This can't be good for his career. No one has officially been called a suspect in her death. Jude remains isolated at the ranch, and I have not seen nor heard from him since that day in the kitchen. I hope they get Hank Greene soon. I'm ready to go on with my life and get this all over with.

Iris is now prepared to claim Margaret's body. After a lot of soul searching, she has made the gut-wrenching determination. "Sonny, I've made the decision not to abandon my mother. I have many more questions than answers about her, but I couldn't live with myself if I don't give the woman a proper burial. I won't walk out on anyone, regardless of the circumstances." Part of the coroner's autopsy will determine if Margaret is Iris's real mother. Hopefully then Iris will be able to heal from the tragedy.

Once her decision is made it doesn't take long to arrange the meeting with the coroner's office. Iris asks me to attend the meeting with her. "Sonny, Peter can't bring himself to go with me. He's angry, and I can't do this alone. Fish just flat refuses."

I am more than happy to go with Iris. I hope that she gets some answers that will help begin to ease her mind. The coroner is a young doctor but very confident. He tells us both that Margaret died from head trauma, but it wasn't from the fall. I assumed like everyone else that her head was hit on the rocks as she tumbled down to the bottom of the ravine. He continues, "The head trauma happened from some type of blunt object, but it wasn't from the rocks. The object was imprinted on her skull and well defined. The police are aware and have the murder weapon in their custody." That caught both of our attentions. Neither of us was aware of a murder weapon.

Unfortunately he was not at liberty to discuss any further details regarding the actual type of weapon and apologizes to Iris for his frankness about the homicide. He knows this hasn't been easy for her, and he is very sympathetic to her situation.

Iris soberly asks something that has troubled her. "Did she freeze to death?"

"She didn't die immediately, but at some point she was probably rendered unconscious from the initial blows to her head," the doctor answers.

Iris and I both gasp and hold each other's hand.

"The wind chill that day was sub-zero, and I can say that she died from her head wounds and not because of the weather. We cannot precisely confirm an exact time of death because of the cold weather conditions, but I can assure you, ladies, this was no accident. She was struck several times on the back of her head very hard. New bruising began to surface around her wrists and ankles." He explains that her body was so badly bruised from the thirty-foot fall into the ravine that the ligature patterns did not appear until several hours later. He concluded the pattern of bruising found confirms that she was restrained at some point in time." He takes a breath. "The substantiation of any sexual assault is inconclusive. She recently engaged in sexual intercourse, but I can't confirm whether it was consensual or rape. There is nothing to suggest sexual trauma."

We both look at each other curiously, but don't say a word. We are both in a state of unease and bafflement.

I look at Iris and know that she's getting ready to pop the big question. "Doctor, is she my natural mother?"

There's a dead silence. The coroner is sifting through Margaret's chart. Iris and I sit patiently waiting to hear the results.

"Miss Bell, the reports confirm that Margaret Beck is your biological mother."

Iris is relieved to know the truth. He lets us know what the next steps will be and escorts us out of his office. He tells us that Margaret's body will be transferred to Raleigh. "This is considered a capital murder case, and they take over now." The transfer of her remains to the state pathology lab makes perfect sense. He continues to say there will be much greater resources, and better advanced equipment at the state lab. They will be able to assist us in finding out who murdered Margaret Beck. The rest is up to the state, and they will contact Iris when Margaret's body is released for pickup. "Thank you for coming in, ladies. Let me know if there is anything else I can do." He leads us out to a reception area and then disappears behind a closed door. Iris is now listed officially as Margaret Beck's legal next-of-kin.

The police are still seeking any clues that may help them solve this case. There is now a nationwide manhunt for Hank Greene, and hopefully he's not gotten to far away. The hunt so far has produced very little information that we are aware of, and there is still no mention of the murder weapon. The only thing we know is Hank and Stash got drunk and disappeared after we found Margaret dead in the ravine. Stash hasn't been seen since.

Riley and I have gone every place we could think of hoping to find him ourselves. We drive down to Georgia, and the few friends he has there haven't seen him either. He is still wanted for questioning, and the longer it takes to find him, the guiltier he looks. I'm sure there is an innocent answer to his whereabouts. The police will still keep looking for him until he shows up and explains everything. Hank never did return to the ranch, and so far that makes him the only suspect to me. The police talked to Fish, and he is furious. They don't want him to leave the area until everything is cleared up. The police have officially cleared Jude from any wrongdoing, and he is no longer considered a person of interest. Jude is honoring the police's request and staying to himself until Hank is apprehended. I wait patiently for things can get back to the way they were just a few short weeks ago.

Peter is in a bad mood all of the time now, and he's not talking to anyone. I have not seen this side of him, and he sure isn't helpin' the situation with Iris at all. Peter totally frustrates me. I don't know what he's got to be so upset about. Nothing has really changed for him. Iris needs him more than she needs me. What is his problem? There have been hints over the years that he may have a hidden edginess to him, but Iris has never said anything. A long time ago she told me that Peter has a hard time gettin' over Vietnam and has terrible nightmares. She said the whole time he was "in country" all he dreamt about was gettin' back home to normalcy. Iris Bell and Why Worry are that normalcy for Peter Benjamin.

Iris renders a heartfelt sentiment. "He went to war as a child and came home an angry man." She is the only one that truly understands him.

I can't even pretend to grasp how Peter must feel. "Iris, I know that millions of people all over the country share his feelin's about the war. Maybe he needs to get some kind of counselin' to help him put this behind him." I'm personally torn in my own opinion. I have friends that have been deeply impacted on both sides of the issue, so I don't judge anyone for their feelings about the war. As a woman I can't be drafted, but I did consider the Navy at one time in my life. I thought about becoming a nurse, and was told by several people that the Navy has the best nursin' school in the country. I'm disappointed on many occasions about my choice not to go, and it's maybe my only regret to this day. I missed my shot, and now I'm too old.

CHAPTER SEVEN

Christmas and New Year's come and go without any new revelations or incident. The celebratory mood on the mountain has turned somber. The once festive spirit is replaced with retrospection. I spend Christmas day with Riley and her daddy, Johnny. Riley begs me to go out with her on New Year's Eve, but I just can't muster the frame of mind to celebrate.

I wait day and night for Jude to knock on my door. I'm talking out loud to myself more and more, and these neurotic feelings are drivin' me nuts. "I'm goin' freaking crazy, somethin's gotta break! God, dude, please!" The mountain is quiet at this moment, but it is not long before the police jerk us out of our la-la land. It has only been a few weeks since Margaret's death, but it seems like forever ago. There is still nothing obvious that would give us a glance into Margaret's real life.

Iris is able to sift through many of her personal items, but other than the locket none of them reveal very much information. "I don't know nothin' more! Not a dang thing! It just ain't possible. I surely hope that, Patricia Kay, women can shed some light on Margaret 'cause I ain't got a chance in hell of findin' out nothin'. She clutches the locket. My heart is broken for the youngin'. Iris hasn't been able to find any of Margaret's family but may have found a possible acquaintance from years ago. "Ya know Iris, that women may be your best bet. Don't give up darlin'." Margaret's house sits just as it was when she died. The yellow tape is broken on the front door, but is still visible. Iris has placed ads in local newspapers down in Florida trying to find any trace of her past, but there haven't been any responses. She is focused on finding someone, anyone who knows Margaret Beck. We're all waiting for any new tidbits of information from the police, but so far we're still no closer to the truth. As the days go by, a veil of tension blankets White Rock Mountain.

I spend my days readin' and piddlin' around the house. Riley is lyin' low, and I still ain't seen Jude. Cabin fever is gettin' the best of me, and I need to get off this mountain. All the uncertainty is nerve-racking. My mind is getting the best of me, and I can't stand the separation from Jude any longer. I jump in the truck and head toward Tessentee. I look for him in passin' but don't catch sight of anyone around the ranch. I just decide to take a drive and end up riding down to Georgia. The further south I travel the weather improves quite a bit, and it feels good to be out of the house. Two hours later I'm in Atlanta, and I don't know what in the heck I'm gonna do now.

I stop at a gas station, use the bathroom, and get a large cup of coffee. I fill my tank with gas and head back to North Carolina. It's a straight shot back home, and it shouldn't take me long. So I hunker down in the seat and listen to all the music I can before my radio goes back to country. I need to get back home before it gets dark, and the melted snow refreezes on the roads. I'm just south of Clayton finally, and I know home is only a short distance away. The sun is setting, and my timin' is perfect. I should get home before dark. My eyes are gettin' tired, and I'm ready to get out of this truck. My butt is sore and numb. The large coffee I purchased is wearin' off, and now I need to pee. The last miles seem like forever long, but the North Carolina border is close.

Out of nowhere the truck suddenly becomes hard to handle. "What the heck?" I realize that my back tire is flat. My truck is an old sixties Chevy and can be a handful during a flat tire. I manage to get stopped and pull off onto the side of the road. I get out and look at it. I have a spare, but standing up and the cold air makes me need to pee. I keep toilet paper in my truck for just such an occasion and retrieve the roll from the glove box. I've got to use the bathroom before I get started changing the tire. Thankfully it's almost dark, and there are very few cars on the highway. I walk down a small embankment next to the truck with my toilet paper in hand. I walk towards some tall bushes and get ready to squat. I struggle in the cold to get my britches down. Just when I get squatted and start to pee, somebody pulls in behind my truck with their bright lights on. I hear a door shut then foot steps going toward my truck.

I frantically try to pull up my jeans, but I can't stop peein'. The footsteps move over to the passenger side of my truck, and through the bushes I can see a man standing next to my truck. A kind voice in the dark calls out. "Sonny, are you down there?"

Oh my God! It's Jude! My fretfulness gets the best of me, and I lose my balance. I fall backward right on top of an open tin can covered by snow and cut the crap out of my butt. I feel warm blood running down my leg. Thank God for toilet paper.

I implore Jude to stay on the bank. "I'm takin' a pee, and I'll be right up Jude." I manage to get everything under control after wallowin' in the trash on the side of the road. I put myself together and join Jude standing next to my truck.

"Hey, Jude, what are you doin' out tonight? I appreciate you stoppin'."

He isn't sure if he should be worried or laugh judging by my looks. I move the hair out of my face and pretend that my butt doesn't hurt like crazy mad. "I must look like I've just wrestled a bear in those bushes. I drank coffee all the way home from Atlanta."

Jude stops my ramblings and laughs. "I seen your truck parked on the side of the road with a flat. I stopped to make sure you were okay and see if you needed help changing your tire."

The timing couldn't be worse. I look horrible, and my butt may need stitches. What more could a man want in a woman, right? Thankfully it's dark, and my oversized coat covers a multitude of mishaps. I appreciate his help.

Its takes him only a few minutes to get the tire changed, and I walk him to his truck when he's finished. "Thanks so much, Jude. Seems like your always comin' to my rescue."

There is a pause, and he doesn't say anything. I look into his eyes and wait to hear any words about us, but they don't come. His actions, though kind, are not what I was hoping for, and my heart is broken. I try to speak, but the words will not come out. We share reserved pleasantries and a hug that almost feels like good-bye. He kisses my cheek, and then my forehead, but never my lips. Before I realize it, Jude is driving away.

I feel like I have just made a colossal mistake of some kind. Somethin' isn't right, and I'm not sure what's goin' on. What has happened since that day in the kitchen?

I fantasized about the next time we see each other again. He scoops me up in his arms and holds me tight. He showers me with declarations of everlasting love and affection. Boy, was I wrong.

The last miles up Tessentee road take forever. Tears rolling down my face make it hard to see in the dark. The roads have icy patches but are still manageable. The trip took much longer than expected, and I dread going home to a cold house. I haven't ever thought about checking into some cheap motel, but the thought of a nice warm room, hot shower, and watching some television sounds really appealing right now. Tempting as that is right now, I am dog-tired, and I don't have the energy to even drive to a motel.

The fire has burned out in the wood stove. The house is so cold that I can see my breath in the air. The moon is dark tonight, but I manage to find and light a kerosene lamp. I glance around the room and make my way over to the woodstove. There are no coals left, but I easily get a new fire restarted. It'll take a few minutes to warm up, and then I can warm some water to clean the gash on my butt.

I carefully peel off my dirty wet jeans and take a look at my rear end in the mirror. I am able to see the damage after several contortions in front of the mirror. The cut is a couple of inches long and pretty darn deep. It's still bleeding pretty heavily, but I'm hopin' that bandages will stop it without havin' to go get any stitches. I could probably use a few, but I'm too wiped out to care.

I carefully wash my wound when the water finally warms up. I clean it out with peroxide afterward and place a large gauze bandage on it. My pajamas have never felt so good. The pain of lying down on the bed immediately reminds me of what a dope I am. I should have never left the cabin today. If I stayed home none of this would have happened. I wouldn't have run into Jude, and my perfect fantasy reunion would, at least in my mind, still be alive. The house is finally startin' to warm up, and I am giving up the fight to stay awake.

My dreams turn violent at some point during the night. Suddenly I am in an unknown town. I go from person to person, begging and pleading for anyone to help me get home. I'm not sure why, but I feel frightened and desperate. I recognize people in my dream.

Jude, Iris, Peter, Stash, Fish, and even Margaret Beck ignore my pleas for help. I can't convince any of them to make it easy for me to get home. I have no money, and no matter how hard I try I can't get home. I sense that I am too far away to walk. I have a car, but I can't find it. When I do finally find my car, it's in hundreds of small pieces. Paralyzed, I can't move. Sobbing and screaming for help doesn't work. I am so tired, and all I want to do is close my eyes for just a few minutes. I meander down a myriad of alleyways. I search frantically for a safe place to close my eyes and sleep. Strange people come out of the dark, and everyone I encounter adds another layer of terror. I cry so hard that I'm huffing in my sleep. I can't stop it, and I can't wake up.

I hear a female voice speaking to me. "Sonny, Sonny, wake up."

I struggle to focus. I'm still crying.

"Sonny, wake up!"

Suddenly, I'm slowly starting to come out of my dread and horror, and finally Riley shakes me out of the night terror.

"Oh, Riley, I had the worst dream ever!"

"It's okay, You're havin' one of those nasty bad dreams again."

"Riley, what time is it?"

She says it's late, but not time to get up yet. "I was on the mountain and came to crash at your place for the night. I heard you crying for help when I reached the front door. I wasn't sure what was going on. You scared me to death!"

I get up to use the bathroom. It's a chilly trip to the outhouse, but I'm used to it. Most the time I grab a paper towel and just squat somewhere closer. When I return to bed Riley is already asleep, and I climb in next to her.

The cold wakes me up this morning. "Dang, this place is frosty!" I've known it for a while, but I just wouldn't get myself up to do anything about it.

Riley is still sleeping. The freezing house doesn't seem to be bothering her at the moment. I can see my breath in the air, so I know it's real chilly. I find any piece of extra clothing within reach and start layering up. The fire has only been out for a few hours, so it shouldn't be difficult to get another one started right away. I get a pot of coffee, and a pan of water going on my camp stove in the kitchen. I don't want to wait for the woodstove to heat up. I feel grungy and would dearly love a hot bubble bath right now. I have an old-fashioned claw tub outside in my yard. I jokingly and lovingly call it my hillbilly hot tub. It sits over a fire pit so I can take a hot bath any time of the year. It's a lot of work to fill and heat in the winter, and I don't have an ounce of energy this morning to even ponder the thought.

I need Riley to look at my wound; it hurts a lot. I peel the gauze dressing back that I put on it last night and look at my rear end in a mirror. I can't believe how bad it looks. I am grabbing my butt cheek and twisting myself to see the gash better.

She wakes up and sees the cut. "what the hell happened to your ass?"

I tell her the story of last night, and all she does is laugh. "I don't know what is so funny, Riley Stone. It hurts like crap."

She helps me clean it with warm water and then boil it out with peroxide. We can't find another bandage in the house anywhere. Riley comes up with a great solution, and goes to the bedroom. I laugh when I see what is in her hands when she returns. She's wavin' around a Kotex and places it over the cut like a bandage. It happens to work out as a perfect replacement for a bandage. Best of all, she uses a small piece of duct tape to hold it on. "Now that's a real hillbilly bandage! I've got to stock up on first aid supplies next time I get to town." It may look ridiculous, but it really cushions my butt when I sit down.

I can't help but break down while we're drinking our coffee. Tears well up in my eyes, and She thinks it is cause of my sore butt. "No, it ain't the cut. It's Jude." I tell her about everything that happened yesterday. "I'm so bummed out, and for the life of me, I don't understand what's happened."

She's a good listener, and sits quietly for me to finish.

"I know there was chemistry when we kissed, and I know what he said to me in the kitchen after Margaret died. What's going on?"

In all of her infinite wisdom she responds. "all this crying over a guy does not suit you. I haven't ever seen you like this! If it's meant to be, then my grannies, it'll happen."

There is hard knock on the kitchen door just as she finishes relaying her words of wisdom. I whisper,

"Hush, I'm not expectin' anyone. Sneak around the corner, and check it out."

I hear her open the kitchen door, but I don't hear any voices. "Who is it, ?" There is no response, and when I stand up to see what's going on, Jude walks around the corner. "Jude!" I stand up too quickly and wince from the pain.

He's dumbfounded by my situation and helps me sit back down. He has no idea what happened yesterday when I was relieving myself in the bushes.

Riley can't help herself and pops off. "She fell back in a snow bank and cut her ass on an ol' jagged tin can last night. That's when you caught her pissin' in the bushes."

I could disappear under this sofa right now.

Jude looks at me. "Oh, ouch, I'm so sorry. You didn't say anything about it last night."

Riley grins at me.

"Okay! Okay! All right, both of you, I'm fine." I can tell Riley is getting ready to take off now that Jude is here. It's not long before she gathers her stuff and heads toward the door.

"Honey can I get anythin' for you before I leave?"

I look at Jude and then at Riley. "I don't need a thing, my dear. I'll be just fine. You go on." I stop her before she can get out the door. "Oh, thanks for the help with my bandage." She gives me the thumbs up and takes off down the steps to her truck.

Jude glances at me, shakes his head, and sits down next to me on the sofa.

"What's up, Jude?" Nervous tension fills the air, and all I can think about is how grungy I am. I reposition myself on the couch. I need to shift the weight off the left side of my butt. "Please excuse the way I look. I'm in desperate need of a hot bath. The last few days ain't been kind to me."

Jude looks at me and smiles. He doesn't answer my question. Instead he says, "You're welcome to use my bathtub." He has all the amenities of comfort including electricity, hot water, and a bathtub.

Taken aback at first by his suggestion, I can't possibly refuse his offer. "Jude, a hot bath sure sounds good right now, then will you please tell me what's goin' on? With us, if there is a you and me? Jude, is there is an 'us'?"

His blue eyes look directly into mine with a vulnerability that I have never seen before. "I'll tell you tonight at dinner. I have to work at the office all day, and you'll have the whole place to yourself."

Well, it didn't take two seconds. "Yes, that would be so groovin' right now. All right, yes, I'll take you up on that." I grab some clean clothes and pack some personal items in a small bag. "Jude, are you tryin' to save me again?"

He assures me that he is not in anyway trying to save me today. "Think of it as neighborly."

I'm not happy with "neighbor," but the hot bath wins my heart over.

Jude's place is located just off the stables. The dÈcor astounds me when I walk through the door. I wasn't sure what to expect, but this was definitely not it. He notices the expression on my face. "Sylvia Graham decorated this place, and just about everything in here belongs to them."

"I can't help it, Jude. This is the fanciest home place I've ever laid eye's on. You actually live here?" The furniture is expensive and beautiful. I can feel the peacefulness immediately when I walk in. Sun fills the large entrance to his home, and I can just about stand up in the huge stone fireplace. My whole cabin would fit in his livin' room.

Jude walks me to the bathroom and acquaints me with the operation of the fancy tub. He hands me a clean robe and some towels from the linen closet. He smiles and politely excuses himself just as promised. "Sonny, I have a few hours of paperwork to do. I'll be back then. Make yourself at home, and I'll see you later for dinner. There's a lot we need to talk about."

I observe him walking through the house and then hear a heavy wooden door shut behind him. I am in awe of this place. If this is the stable house, I can't imagine what the main house must look like. This bathroom is unbelievable, and the tub is big as a swimming pool. The view out the bathroom window is spectacular, and the grounds are kept to perfection.

Pasture and distant mountain ranges surround my view from the tub. This is a true luxury, and I will take my time enjoyin' every minute of it. There is a television actually in the bathroom, so I turn it on just to see what I've been missin'. President Ford may not win re-election because he pardoned Richard Nixon after his impeachment. It doesn't take me long to turn it off. I could fall asleep in the bathtub looking out the window.

White Rock Mountain is usually my sanctuary away from all of the bad news that fills the airwaves, but the murder of Margaret really hits close to home. Is there any place that is sacred anymore?

I literally have to climb out of the tub it's so big. The robe has the scent of Jude when I put it on. I haven't slept much in days, and my eyes are heavy. The bath relaxed me, and I decide to use this time to take a brief nap. I hesitate to lie down on his bed, but it looks so comfortable. His bed covering is goose down, and I melt into a little piece of heaven when I slide under the bedspread. This is a great bed. Maybe the best bed I have ever slept on. It doesn't take long, and I drift off.

The smell of food cooking wakes me up. I jump off the bed and put on the clean clothes that I packed earlier. I put on a little make-up and blow my hair dry. I meander out to the kitchen when I feel presentable. Tonight's important, and I want to look my best. It's been a long time since I put on make-up for a man. There is a fire burning in the big fireplace, and I notice that it's already gettin' dark outside.

Jude is in the kitchen cooking dinner. The great smells are makin' me hungry. He didn't hear me come out of the bedroom and is startled when I speak to him. "What time is it, ? How long have I been sleeping?" I notice a clock, and it's five o'clock. I have slept for almost five hours. "Why didn't you wake me?" I still feel physically and emotionally exhausted, but I didn't mean to sleep so long.

"I couldn't, you were sleeping too peacefully." He has the table set for dinner, and sweetly motions me to sit down. "You're just in time. "There is an open bottle of wine, and he pours me a glass. I don't usually drink, but I do enjoy a glass of wine with dinner now and then. Shots of tequila with lime and salt were my drink of choice when I was young. "How do you feel, ?"

"I feel great. Thanks so much, it's been a great day. Everything looks fantastic, and the food smells wonderful. A girl could definitely get used to this." I pinch myself to make sure that I'm not in a dream.

At dinner Jude opens up and finally explains what happened after Margaret's death. "Sonny, I need to start by saying that I knew nothing about this when I came here with Hank Greene." Turns out Hank has a significant violent past, and a couple of felony assault charges back in Idaho. One was against a man, and the other a woman. Both of them barely survived the brutal attacks, but he spent five years in prison for the vicious assaults. "Hank Greene is an awful man, the police suspected him in Margaret's death early on, and I was asked to secretly help bring him into custody alive. He needs to face his punishment and is going to have a long time to do so."

I believe every word Jude is saying, and a sense of relief washes over me. I listen to the rest of the story with intense attention.

"Sonny, I swear to God, I was kept under surveillance for the last few weeks. They were following me back to Franklin the night I seen you one the road, and I couldn't say anything. I had been down in Clayton to hook up with Hank. The police wanted me to wear a wire and tape my conversation with him, hoping to get a confession. We really thought that I was going to flush him out of hiding, but he never did show. I was on my way home last night." The police are sure that Hank will try and contact Jude and that he is still in the area. "Sonny, Hank has disappeared into thin air, and I'm gonna get him. I brought him here, and I'm gonna get him."

The Grahams have been great throughout this whole thing. They are scared but feel confident that Hank will be arrested soon for Margaret's murder.

"Jude, I'm curious. Where in the heck did you meet him?"

They met in Texas at a large cattle ranch. Jude had worked with an oil-drilling outfit, but the job didn't last long. "I've known Hank Greene for a couple of years. He came with me when it was time to move on from the cattle ranch. I saw an AD for the Grahams' job in an Austin paper. I was hired by the Grahams after several long distance phone conversations. Hank just came along, hoping for a job too. James and Sylvia hired him based on my recommendation."

I always thought Hank was the boss. "Jude, if the police are sure he's the killer, then what about Stash and Fish?"

He told me Stash was found at an old girlfriend's house. He went there the night of Margaret's death and stayed on till after the holidays. "Sonny, he's home, but you just haven't seen him. Fish was also cleared of any charges the other day. Last I heard he was heading to London for a concert."

That's great news for both of 'em. The whole time Jude is talking I can see myself with him. He is easy, comfortable, and definitely very attractive. He's the same age as me but looks younger. Jude has been the perfect gentleman today, and it has been a long time since I have felt this way about anyone. The wine is making me a little tipsy, but I feel great. When we're done eating dinner, Jude and I make ourselves comfortable on the oversized sofa that faces the fireplace. I have not thought about anyone or anything else all day. It's the first time in weeks. Jude is capturing my heart, and I enjoy his company immensely. I feel vulnerable and safe in his arms. He's a big man, and it's easy to get lost in his embrace. Out of nowhere and unexpectedly it begins to thunder. Incredibly the sky opens up, and the snow starts pouring down. Jude calls it "thunder snow."

Concern about the cabin raises my anxiety, and I have to make a terrible decision. "Jude, this has been a glorious day and evenin'." He stops me with a kiss before I can complete my sentence. "You're very convincin'! I've been gone for hours and should probably scoot home. I'm sure the fire is out and the house is cold." I look out the window; the snowflakes are big and beautiful. "The snow looks pretty intense. I'd love to stay, but I better get up the gap before it piles up much higher. Do you mind givin' me a ride home?" Kissing me throughout my entire conversation has only made my decision to head home much more difficult, and it's really hard to leave.

The weather report was predicting a good bit of snow. Sadly he knows I'm gettin' anxious and agrees to take me home. The ranch is not to far away, but Hickory Gap Road can be dangerous if the weather gets too bad. He is a perfect gentleman and warms the truck.

We're ready to go within minutes. I take one quick glance around his house. "I think I've got everything." I stop Jude to kiss him before we head out the door. "I'm sorry to spoil this great day and evening, but I can't relax when there is somethin' worryin' me. I'm sure the cabin is probably fine, but I'd feel better to see it for myself."

Jude returns the kiss with a strong hug. "Sonny, I'd do anything for you."

We see Stash trudging up the road on our way to my place. His friends probably dropped him off down on Tessentee. Jude stops and offers to give him a ride the rest of the way home, and he jumps in next to me. He's obviously intoxicated, but congenial enough. We share small talk and niceties, but the subject of Margaret's murder never comes up, so I make the decision to bring up the subject in the awkward conversation, "I am so glad to see you, Stash. I knew you didn't have anything to do with Margaret." "Hey, thanks ya'll! That whole scene was terrible. Ya know, Margaret was a good women. If I get my hands on Hank Greene, he won't see the inside of a courtroom cause I'll put him under the courthouse! Man, that dude just ain't right!"

Jude lightly squeezes my hand. Daniel is still living in his camper, buts stays away with friends quit a bit in the winter. There hasn't been much more progress on his cabin. The winter stopped him in his tracks.

The gap is pretty hard to drive, and Jude decides to drive Stash home first. He has chains on his truck tires and makes it seem easy hauling us up the mountain. The snow is still pouring down like rain, and it doesn't seem to be stopping anytime soon. Stash hugs me before he gets out. "I'll come visit soon."

I return the nicety and watch till he gets in the door. We head toward my place. Jude makes it up my hill without too much trouble. He gets out and walks me the door.

I love the way he looks at me.

"I'll come by and see you tomorrow, Sonny Branch."

I fumble for the keys and then somehow manage to unlock the door. "I can't wait, Jude Turner." I make it into the house, and he steps inside to take a quick glance around. "All appears well, Mr. Turner. Don't worry about me. I'll be fine!"

The great anticipated kiss goodnight proves to be breathtaking, and my heart is beatin' out of my chest. I shut the door. He waits to hear the door lock before he leaves.

The snow is pilin' up quick, and Jude has a distance to go before he can get back home. Good thing it's all downhill. I light a nearby glass lantern and then a fire. Luckily, I chopped a lot of wood this fall and have an abundant supply. My mind is racin', and I doubt much sleep is in my near future. The last time I went to Franklin, I picked up a good book at the library, and tonight will be the perfect night start on it. I set a kettle on the woodstove for some hot tea, and the cabin is startin' to warm up faster then I thought it would. I briefly glance at my cut in the mirror I have on my closet door. It feels better, but it still looks horrible. I put another Kotex over my poor wound and slip into my pajamas. I take a few minutes to brush my hair out, and the teakettle is hot. I get ready for a great night of reading. I feel at peace tonight, and for the first time in a long time it seems like everything is really lookin' up. The wind is starting to pick up, and the snow is gusting sideways. I have no way of knowin' if Jude made it home okay, but I feel confident that he probably did. I think about everyone on the mountain, and shout out a pithy prayer for all of 'em. I doze off on the sofa reading my book.

CHAPTER EIGHT

An unfamiliar noise wakes me up. I lie there for a minute, and then I hear it again. It's comin' from the bedroom, but I can't make out the sound. My .38 pistol is lyin' on the table next to me. I quietly pick it up and stand. I'm frightened, but the last time this happened there was a raccoon outside my window.

My bedroom is dark so I can't make out anything in particular just looking in there. The only light is the very small flicker of a lantern in the livin' room, and a small fire in the woodstove. It's shinin' a teeny amount of light into the room, but not enough to make a big difference. The curtains are open, but the clouds are covering any chance of moonlight. I slip over to the dresser and get my flashlight. Then I ease over to the window. I shine the light outside. Nothing is out there. I wave the flashlight in a sweepin' motion over the ground, but I still don't see anything. I shine the flashlight around my bedroom, and don't see anything out of the ordinary. It must have been the wind.

The sound of something fallin' in my closet surprises me. I point my gun towards the closet, and shout out. "I have a gun!" Then I ask, "Riley is that you? This isn't funny, Riley."

I'm shaking now, and the gun is startin' to get heavy in my hands. A loud thud from the closet reinforces my apprehension. "If you're someone I know, you best speak now, cause I will shoot ya!" I pull back the hammer. The noise is unmistakable, but there is still no movement or attempt to surrender. I can hear heavy breathing filterin' through the door. "Come out or I'll shoot! I mean it!"

Slowly and steadily I edge over to grab the doorknob. The person in my closet is startled when I swing open the door and immediately lunges towards me. I'm knocked down to the floor, and there's a man on top of me. He is struggling and desperately tryin' to wrestle the gun from my hand. He's wearing a black ski mask, dark clothing, and his breath has the stench of stale beer and cigarettes. Before he is able to completely over power me, I shoot him. The bullet pierces his chest at close range, and I can smell the gunpowder.

The gunshot temporarily deafens me, and the weight of him crashes down on top of me. I'm not sure if he's dead. He ain't movin'. I struggle to crawl out from underneath him. All of a sudden massive power and strength over takes my body. I hoist him off, and he rolls onto his back. I see smoke comin' from his chest, and I'll never forget the putrid smell.

The first thing I do is remove his facemask, and I can't believe who it is: Hank Greene I check to see if he has a pulse, and he does. His breathin' is shallow and slow, and he is barely alive. I lift his upper body into my lap so his head is resting upright on my chest. "Hank, Hank, what in the hell are you doin' in my house?"

His eyes are open, and he looks at me with terror and fear. Blood is gurgling from his mouth, but he is murmuring. "I can't hear you. Just hold on." I have to get some help, and for the first time I regret not havin' a telephone. What was he freaking thinkin'?

I don't have time to worry about it right now. Hank is dyin' before my eyes, and won't last till I run to get help. Sitting on the floor with Hank in my lap, there is a cold realization. There's nothin' I can do. The only thing left to do is stay and pray with him.

It takes only a few minutes, and I am sure he has passed. Sobbing, shaking, and covered in his blood, I sit in the dark with his dead body in total disbelief. I mumble to myself, "Sonny, snap out of it, you have to go get help! I've gotta get help!" I repeat the words over and over, but I sit paralyzed on the floor unable to move.

I scramble to find the flashlight when I do finally get wits about me. I leave Hank, jump in the truck, and head out into the snowstorm. I need to get to the ranch and find Jude. Thank God for small favors. The snow has slowed. The road has many inches covering it, and I don't have chains on my tires. If I can make it to Jude's, he can call for help.

There are limbs down, but thankfully no trees so far. The worst curve in the road is steep, and will prove to be my biggest obstacle. I can easily end up in the ditch if I lose control goin' down and around the sharp curve. The intensity to reach Jude at all costs gives me no option but to forget the reality of what just happened. I shot and killed a man in my house. Not just any man, but Hank Greene!

By the grace of God I reach the stables, and lay on the truck horn as I approach his house. I see his lights come on, and Jude comes running out to meet me.

"Jude, there was a man. I heard a man in my bedroom closet. I warned him that I was armed and begged him to come out. No one came out, Jude, and I knew someone was in there. I opened the door. He lunged towards me, and I shot him. He's dead, Jude. He's dead."

He has a firm grip on me, and helps hold me up so I can walk to the house. "Jude, the man hiding in my bedroom closet was Hank Greene! Please, please, call the police!" This whole scene is just like my nightmares. Jude tries to sit me down. "No, we have to call the police! Hank is dead, and I killed him!" I notice the telephone and run to it. I call the police to report the shooting. "My name is Sonny Branch. I live up here on Hickory Gap Road. There was a man in my house tonight, and I shot and killed him. His name is Hank Greene, he's wanted by the police, and I need someone to come up to my place."

The voice on the other end reassures me that she will immediately dispatch officers to my house.

Jude fully realizes what is happening.

"Jude, we have to get back up to the cabin."

"Sonny, I'll go. You stay here."

An unyielding look came over my face. "No, ! It's my house, my bedroom, my gun, and *I* killed Hank. There is no way on God's green earth that you're gonna stop me from going back home! Besides that, the police will want to know what the hell happened!"

The look of angst and horror on my face convinces Jude he is no match for me. When we arrive back at the cabin, there is a trace of light coming from the living room window. There's still a small fire burnin' in the woodstove. The snow has stopped for the moment, and from outside the cabin looks cold and evil.

"He's in my bedroom on the floor."

Jude tells me to wait in the truck. "I'll go check everything out first. The police will be here soon." He kisses me on the cheek and jumps out with his flashlight.

When Jude gets inside the door he's careful not to disrupt anything in the house. He learned a lot when Margaret Beck died. He sees his old friend lyin' on the floor and goes to his side. Though he is still warm to the touch, Jude knows that he is dead. "Hank, what in the heck were you doing in Sonny's house tonight? Why didn't you let me help you?"

Within minutes he returns to the truck, and confirms what I already knew. "Hank is dead." The full weight of what I have done is crashing down around me, and Jude holds me tight. "I can't go back into that house. Not yet! Not right now!" He turns up the heat in the truck, and we sit silently waiting for the cops. There are no questions, no judging, and no blaming, just utter and complete silence.

I notice that Hank's blood is drying on my hands, face, and clothing. Jude still maintains his tight hold of me. "I love you."

The words escaped my lips, and I can't believe what I just uttered. I don't want him to answer, cause I may not like what I hear. I redirect the conversation before he has a chance to respond.

He holds my face tenderly in his hands. "Sonny, Sonny, look at me." He gently turns my cheek so I can see his eyes, and the red lights of the police cars interrupt us. "We will finish this conversation later."

The police arrive quickly despite the snow storm. I look directly into Jude's eyes and speak to him before he gets out of the truck. "This is real! Not a nightmare! I killed a man tonight!"

I'm struck with panic, and it's worsening. I can't sit in the truck. I jump out of the truck to walk my fear off in the cold air. "Keep your head together. Hank was in the wrong. There is no way this is your fault."

A police officer stays behind with me outside, and his partner goes in the house with Jude. "Ma'am, I know you've had a hell of a night. I hate to put you through this, but I need to know everything that happened here tonight. Would you be more comfortable telling your story in the house?"

I can tell he is cold and would rather be inside. I take a deep breath and head toward the front door. There is another police car coming up the gap, followed by an ambulance. Jude promises me that everything will be all right once I am inside. The paramedics enter the house with their own flashlights and emergency equipment.

I can only hear pieces of conversation taking place around me. I feel like I'm in a haze or in slow motion.

My hearing still hasn't returned, and noise sounds like it is comin' through a long tunnel. I realize someone is talking to me, and it's Jude. "Don't worry about anything. Shooting Hank was justified. He could have killed you. I repeat, this is not your fault!"

Hank has been the main suspect in the death of Margaret Beck. Since then Fish, Stash, and Jude have been exonerated. The truth be told he was probably the only serious suspect they ever really considered.

"Jude, please stay with me while I tell my side of the story."

Hank's body lies a room away. Jude puts another log on the fire and starts the kettle for tea. One of the officers comes out of the bedroom with my gun in a plastic bag. "That's the gun I used to kill him. I have a permit, and the gun is legal."

The two detectives that have been working with Jude on Hank's case walk in the door. "We heard about the shooting. Sonny, are you okay?"

I answer civilly and point in the direction of where Hank is lyin'. One of the detectives takes a seat close to where I'm sittin'. Jude brings me a hot cup of tea and sits besides me on the sofa. "Okay, darlin', start at the beginning." Jude calling me darling didn't fall on my almost deaf ears. His kindhearted attention makes it easier to recount the horrible event.

"Detective, I killed Hank Greene! I shot and killed him!"

"Wait, wait, and slow down. Miss Branch, start with when you got home tonight."

Jude looks at the detective and then gives me a reassuring squeeze.

"Jude brought me home around seven this evenin'. The cabin was dark, and I immediately lit the hurricane lanterns. I started a fire and went to the bedroom. "The horror of Hank Greene in my closet has just hit me. "Jude! Jude! He watched me undress. He watched me look at the gash on my butt in the mirror. He saw me naked!" My stomach is in knots, and the stress has started a severe and throbbin' headache. I grab my head in pain. "Jude! I'm gonna puke!" I break out in a severe cold sweat, and water is pouring off every inch of my body.

Jude jumps right in and starts to care for me. The paramedic takes a look at me and determines that it is not life threatening. Jude tells me the massive headache is from the all tension and trauma. "Baby girl, you're gonna be all right. Try to calm down." He soothingly wipes my face with a cool, wet cloth.

The detective gives us a few minutes so I can collect my thoughts. He joins the others in the bedroom. They're ready to take Hank out of the house.

I watch 'em carry his body in a black bag on a stretcher through my living room, and out the door. I thought it would be hard to watch, but instead I have feelings of anger, repulsion, and disgust for the man. "Jude, I'm glad I killed him. I will never forgive him for what he's done to Margaret."

The detective needs me to answer a few last questions, and they will be finished for the night. "Detective, I fell asleep readin' a book. A noise woke me up. I thought it might be a critter or somethin' outside. When I heard it again I was standin' in the bedroom, and the noise was comin' from my closet. I warned whoever was in there that I had a gun, and I would shoot. No one said anything. When I went to open the door a man—I mean, Hank—lunged at me, knocking me down on the floor. We wrestled, and I shot him."

Jude is starting to get angry hearing me recount the story. He feels responsible for bringing Hank to the mountain. "Sonny, I just never knew. I swear!"

The detective refocuses our conversation. "I can tell you that you are one lucky lady tonight. Hank Greene may be responsible for several sexual assaults in at least four states that we know of. He is a brutal monster, a serial rapist, and you stopped him. My only question is why he spared you. He had ample time, but for some reason he changed his mind. That's curious and fortunate for you." Apparently, he was in my closet all evening, maybe all day. I never had a clue until I heard the scuttle. They think he hid there waiting for me to fall asleep. I'm less of a threat if caught off guard.

I listen closely to every word he is saying.

"When he knocked some stuff over in the closet you woke up, and you had a gun. Neither of which he was probably expecting. This is his technique and pattern."

I can't help but feel that Margaret Beck really gave him a run for his money the day he waited for her in the dark. Regrettably, Margaret wasn't nearly as blessed as I have been. I am relieved, but the fact remains that I killed another human being. There is a consensus ren-

dered for now anyway, and the shooting is ruled justified. I was protecting myself and my property. He was
in my house, and I had every right to shoot and kill
him. They won't be arresting me tonight, and hopefully
not ever. I feel some relief, but it doesn't change the fact
that I killed someone. "Ma'am, we're sorry for the awful
ordeal you suffered. If we need anything else, we'll be
in touch."

The place where Hank lay is blood soaked, and the
smell is atrocious. "Jude, I can't stay here tonight. I just
can't."

Jude agrees. He helps me out to the truck, shuts up
my house, and we head down to the ranch. My legs
can barely carry me towards Jude's front door, and I am
covered in dried blood. Jude lifts me up and carries me
the rest of the way into the house. He gently sets me on
the bed in his spare bedroom.

"Do you think this is the end of it?"

He helps me out of my coat. "I think so, I think so."
He takes my shoes off.

"I killed Hank Greene."

"I know. It's late, and the sun will be up shortly. You
need a hot shower and rest right now. I don't want you
to worry about a thing. I'll go up to the cabin at daylight and take a look around."

Jude was right. The shower felt great, and the sheets
feel even better. He comes in the room to say goodnight.
He pulls the blankets up tight and kisses me sweetly
on the lips. "Jude, we have a plan, and now I just need
some rest and daylight." I hear him agree, but not much
after that. I am exhausted and sleep finally prevails.

I smell fresh coffee brewing and hear the morning news on the television. I look over at the clock, and it's already nine. I jump up out of bed in a tizzy. I call his name a few times and realize he's not here. A note lies next to the coffee pot reassuring me of his eventual return. The sun is out, and the snow is blinding white. I can't completely get out of my stupor, even with fresh coffee. My entire body is still craving sleep. Well, Sonny, you have two options here. I can walk home, or I can lie back down and wait for Jude to get back home. Of course, he may be up at my place. I decide to call Fish instead, and there is no answer. He has already left for London. I call Riley but only speak with her dad. He will let her know that I called. I can't muster up the energy to walk home so I decide to stay and take a short nap. I'll wait for Jude to get home.

I can feel his breath on my neck after what seems like only moments of sleep. His warm hand slowly follows the line of my robed silhouette. He kisses my shoulder and then my neck. My body responds, and I arch my back just slightly to show my pleasure and approval. His passionate kisses move to my mouth.

Extraordinary desire and love unites us, and we become one. His arms surround my body like a glove, and he makes love to me carefully and deliberately. I pull his mouth toward mine. My eyes and lips never leave his. His body is beautiful, and I shudder with every thrust. He is unhurried at first, and then harder and faster. He is physically powerful and seductive. I'm far above the ground, and falling out of the sky all at the same time. There are no other words to describe the way he makes me feel.

My emotions get the best of me when we come to an end, and I can't hold back the tears. Jude wipes them away and doesn't utter a word. I lay in his arms with amazing satisfaction. I lay my face on his chest, and listen to his heartbeat. It's not long before Jude's breathing slows, and I can tell he has fallen asleep.

I leave Jude a fresh pot of hot coffee, a short note, and decide to walk home. It's time to face the nightmare and see what's happened. The sunshine and fresh air will feel good. The walk takes about me an hour in all the snow, but my divine thoughts kept me good company.

When I make it to the last curve of the driveway, I notice that my truck is sittin' exactly where I left it, and there doesn't appear to be anything different from the outside. I dread goin' in and confronting the unspeakable truth. "Well ol' girl, it's time to face your worst night terror ever. I just thought they were in my head, but this was a real life tragedy."

I feel cold air immediately when I open the front door, and the quiet is alarming. I don't smell anything bad, and everything is back in their proper places. I walk into the bedroom. It's full of sunlight and warmth, and everything looks back to normal. The soiled spot where I shot Hank is gone. I realize that Jude must have cleaned the place. I stand frozen in my tracks and think about Hank being inside the closet watchin' my every move. Emotions overwhelm me, and I fall to my knees and pray out loud. "God, please forgive me for what I have done. Please forgive me for takin' another life."

A car door shuts. Iris, Peter, Stash, and Riley come into the bedroom and find me on my knees. I hold back the tears. "I can't believe you guys came. How did you find out?"

Stash helps me up off the floor.

"I killed him you know. I killed Hank. I shot him in the chest at close range. I held him while he died, and there was fear in his eyes." I shed tears for Hank Greene, and I weep for me. "It's regarded as self-defense. You guys heard that, right?"

There is not a dry eye in the place. I wipe my face and blow my nose.

Riley is intent on squeezing me to death. "Dear heart, he was a bad man."

Iris and Peter head to the kitchen after long hugs and kind words of support. Stash is my strong kindred spirit. He is a great source of strength and comfort. My friends are the best, and I am truly blessed to have them in my life.

CHAPTER NINE

Today is Valentine's Day, and the pain of Hank Greene is shrinking. Iris gets word that Margaret's ashes are ready to pick up. She had her cremated when the state released her body. Peter doesn't go with her, so I volunteer to ride along. She plans to keep the ashes for a while, at least until she has decided what to do with them. I don't believe Iris is ready to give her up yet. It's a sad thing for Iris. She found her mother after all these years, and then she lost her because of a warped act of violence by one man. The good news is the police officially charged Hank Greene for the death of Margaret Beck even though he is dead. I am cleared of any wrong doin' in the shooting, and my case is ruled self-defense.

Stash told us that Hank and Margaret had been secretly dating. She attempted to break it off with him. He became outraged and wasn't going to let it end there. Hank was stalking her day and night. Stash didn't know Hank had spiraled so far out of control, and Margaret didn't tell anyone. The last hours of Margaret's life were cruel and painstaking. Stash feels awful for not see-ing the signs. Hank and him drank a lot together, but Stash avows he never saw this comin'. Everyone on the mountain feels responsible for Margaret Beck's death in some small way. There are a lot of would've, could've, should haves going on. The truth be told, none of us ever expected this to happen, and I hope we can all move forward and heal. The clouds that overshadow our beautiful mountain gap are unbearable. We can't catch a break, and I just don't know how much longer any of us can stand it.

Detectives are coming out to Why Worry today. They want to go over the final report with Iris. I knew he was coming, and Iris wanted to make sure I was there when he arrived. The documents he possessed paint a terrifying picture of Margaret's eventual demise. "Miss Bell and Miss Branch, let me be the first say that Hank Greene was a malicious and wicked man, and with that said I'll continue with the report. From what we can tell Hank was able to subdue Mrs. Beck; he tied her up and held her captive for an unknown period of time. The document articulates that Margaret Beck possibly endured hours of torment. The last report of anyone speaking to her was the day before her death. Her phone records show that Samuel Fisher contacted Margaret the night before she died. The rope Hank Greene used was an exact match to the rope he used at the Graham's place.

"I apologize for the graphic nature of the next infor-mation. The murder weapon was a wooden meat-ten-derizing mallet from Mrs. Beck's kitchen. The police found the bloody mallet not far from the crime scene hidden in a metal culvert. The blows to her head with the wooden hammer would have incapacitated her tremendously, but she somehow kept her composure and strength to escape his capture.

"The brutal beatings were done in her basement. Hank made an attempt to clean up the crime scene, but he wasn't very thorough. We followed the blood trail from the house to the ravine where she was found. Mrs. Beck had the wherewithal to try and escape by car, and for some reason that didn't work out, and she found herself outside running for dear life."

Iris and I sit and listen. The detective continues to explain in easy terms what we are looking at and reading. "She would have been confused and easily turned around once outside. How she managed to get so far is almost a miracle. The head wounds that she sustained are inconsistent with further life."

I am left speechless. Iris is almost spent, and I don't know how much more she can take. The detective concludes his summary. "She unfortunately succumbed to her injuries and tumbled off the bank down to the bottom of the ravine."

The notion that she may have called out for help, and lay there in the freezin' cold murmuring for anyone to hear her pleas was an unbearable thought. The doctors notes reassure us she was "probably" dead the entire time she lay down there.

Iris sits in clutching her mother's locket. "Oh my God, Sonny! Oh my God!"

The news of Margaret's death makes it to Florida. All of Iris's ads in the local papers have spurred someone to come forward and may payoff with information for Iris. Iris is at Margaret's house when the phone rings. When the man on the other end started speaking, she is relieved and upset at the same time. She confides in me before telling Peter. "Sonny, a man by the name of Steve Beck is claimin' to be Margaret's natural son."

"Margaret had a son? You have a brother? You have got to be kiddin' me!" Things are finally starting to settle down, and this comes out of the blue.

She is concerned that this Steve Beck may have ulterior motives after speaking briefly to him on the telephone. "Sonny, he doesn't care about her ghastly death or the fact that she is gone. All he cares about is money, and I don't know about any money. Other than her house, I don't know anything. She talked about a small retirement stipend. But I haven't found anyone who can confirm that."

So now we all wait for the immensely anticipated arrival of Mr. Beck. Peter and Iris decide they'll pick him up at the train depot down in Georgia. That will give 'em all time to talk before we bombard him when he arrives to White Rock Mountain. Iris says he has all the legal documents including a birth certificate to verify that he is Margaret Beck's son, Iris and Peter remain vigilant and distrustful of his intentions. Neither of them really knows anything about him, and I hope there suspicions do not come to pass. I try not to prejudge the guy, but it is challenging.

Jude and I are both so thankful to have this terrible ordeal behind us. I couldn't be happier, and Jude is ecstatic. I never thought I was capable of loving, anyone or anything, as much as I love Jude Turner. I just never thought that God's plan for me included finding love again. He is everything I could possibly ever want in a man, and I never thought it would happen at my age.

James and Sylvia Graham are also recovering from all the craziness. The stables are running flawlessly because of Jude. Fish is still overseas, and Stash has been lying low.

Peter has isolated himself at Why Worry, and for the most part Iris has been spendin' her time at Margaret's place. I'm not sure what the deal with that is, but I'll leave it up to Iris to tell me what's goin' on.

This winter has been full of turmoil and mayhem. I'm ready to get off this roller coaster, and ride the merry-go-round for awhile. Jude thinks I should get some kind of counseling for my incident with Hank, but I reject that opinion. "People died, but I didn't die. Margaret suffered unspeakable crimes, and I didn't. For whatever reason Hank didn't hurt me, and he certainly could've if he really wanted to. I am still here. So I have a lot to be thankful for." My night terrors remain, but I've always had them. Now I have a different script. I hate that Hank is dead, but I don't regret pullin' the trigger. I will do it again if I'm ever put in that situation again.

Steve Beck is due to arrive today. Iris and Peter pick him up as planned. We are all getting together later this evening at Margaret's place for a meet and greet. It's gotten really hard to reserve my opinion of the man. I know there are always two sides to every story, but I don't want him messin' with my dear friends Iris and Peter.

My first impression is that he's somewhat older than Iris and seems to be a pretty genuine guy. He tells us very little about Margaret but does say that she and he have been estranged for many years. He doesn't volunteer any more detail even when pressed by questions. He is a smooth talker and is able to spin any story his way. He's tall like his mother, red-headed like Iris, and seems to be in his mid-thirties. He is some type of salesman in aluminum siding or vacuum cleaners. He comes off to be a pretty respectable type guy, but there is definitely unease between him, Iris, and Peter.

I can tell by the look on Iris and Peter's faces that things have not been going so well behind the scenes. They have hid it well, but Steve's presence is wearing on them, and Peter offers to take him to his motel.

I get Iris alone, and she is infuriated. "Sonny, I was dead right. All he wants is money! My sixth sense was right on target! All he came here for was money."

Earlier he took Iris outside, and demanded half the worth of Margaret's place and pension. "I gladly settled on a price just to get rid of him. I wrote him a check, and Peter will be takin' him back to the train station tomorrow. He has no interest whatsoever in his own mother or me." She starts crying uncontrollably. "How did this happen? I have wanted a family my entire life!"

Peter and Steve's ride to town was less than friendly, and the family reunion is fractured before it gets started. There are always two sides to every story, but his actions were cold and insensitive. I hope one day that Iris and her brother will be able to sit down together and talk rationally. They will probably discover that they have a lot more in common than either of them thinks right now.

The tail end of winter is still with us, and everyone on the mountain is getting cabin fever. We're all getting keyed up for spring. It won't be long before this mind-blowing winter is behind us all. Johnny Stone is not weathering well. He's taken a turn for the worse. His health is failin', and Riley is home a lot to care for him. She checks in with all of us from time to time, and we still enjoy an occasional sleep over. I get a telephone. My very first legitimate utility, and I must admit that I love it. I got the message loud and clear when I wasn't able to call for help the night I shot Hank Greene.

I'm not used to havin' the phone, and it still freaks me out when the darn thing rings. Jude, Riley, or Iris is usually on the other end. I'm trying to talk Iris and Peter into gettin' one for Why Worry, but so far they aren't buying into the idea. They had the phone disconnected at Margaret's house and have no plans to get another one.

I have been spending a lot of time writing these days. My recent experiences have renewed my passion, and I can't stop writing them down on paper. I still see

Jude most every day, and we're still crazy about each other. The winter makes his job much more difficult, but he does have a ranch hand now to help him out.

The veterinarian that Hank and Jude were expecting never did show up. The Grahams signed a contract with Christina St. Mark, and she will be movin' out to the ranch soon. I must admit that I have a twinge of jealousy when it comes to Dr. St. Mark, but my faith in Jude supersedes my foolish way of thinkin'. I know he adores me, and I have to fight hard not to question those feelings. Jealousy is an ugly and awful feelin' and doesn't do a thing to improve our relationship. I've had my share of jealousy over the years, and I learned my share of unpleasant lessons too. I put my faith in God and Jude.

The night is cold and dark. I hear footsteps following me close behind, and I run through the woods in panic. I feel the locust thorns slashing my skin, but all I can do is to keep running. I'm struggling to get home, but I can't seem to find it. I emerge out of a dense laurel thicket and realize I'm at Tessentee ranch. "Thank you, Lord!"

Before I can catch my breath, an unknown man comes out from inside the stables. He lifts his gun to shoot me. I take aim back at him and shoot to kill. I see Riley and Iris huddled together behind an out building, but I can't reach them. I reload my pistol when another man appears, and I shoot him dead. Jude is here, but he won't help me. I realize that he is the one that has been following me. I stop and cry out. "Jude! Jude! Please help me!" I can't move, and I tell myself repeatedly.

"Sonny, Sonny, wake up! It's just a bad dream." I say it again and again until I am finally able to stop the dream, and wake up. I practically throw myself out of the bed and onto the floor just to shake it off. I stumble to the kitchen and grab some juice from the cooler. My cottonmouth is really bad this morning, and my tongue is sticking to my uvula. The night terrors are at an all time incredible level of insanity. I wake up more tired than when I went to bed. Finally I start to regain my wits after a swig of juice, and the grogginess is starting to subside.

The mountain has been quiet these past few weeks, thank goodness. I just don't think I could take any more drama in my life right now. Today is Margaret Beck's funeral. Iris has decided to have a memorial service. She is going to keep some of her ashes but will scatter most in the branch that runs along the side of her house. There is a wake afterward at Margaret's home.

I think Margaret would approve of Iris's decisions. She loved this place and wouldn't be happy anywhere else. I only have a few hours till the funeral, and I plan to enjoy what's left of this morning. The phone rings, and Jude is on the other end. "Sonny, I'm really sorry honey, but I can't make it to Margaret's funeral today. Do ya forgive me?"

There is disappointment in my voice. "Oh, Jude, I don't want to go if you're not gonna be there."

"I'm covered up with work. We have a foal on the way, and I can't get away today."

I'm dismayed. "All right, call me later. Love ya."

The phone goes dead. I can hardly hold it against him. This is the first time he has cancelled any of our plans since we started dating.

Fish gives Margaret a superb eulogy. Stash, Iris, and Peter all speak too. Most was antidotal, but it's a true and heartfelt observance of her life. Iris pours her remains into the creek, and a strong gust of wind comes out of nowhere. The current of air spreads her ashes perfectly over the small running creek. The end of the service is a fitting beginnin' to her wake. Iris decides to celebrate Margaret's life, not mourn it. Margaret's home is beautiful. Iris ordered flowers, and the kitchen is full of food and people. I mingle around the house looking for any life treasure's that may give me hints of who this woman really was. There are not many personal items on display, but one picture does capture my attention. Margaret must be in her early twenties. The picture shows a vibrant and beautiful Margaret Beck. Oddly there is nothing else visible that dates back prior to her living in North Carolina. Neither Iris nor Peter has been able to find out much.

Peter spends most of his time upset with Iris. I know he hurts for her deeply, but he needs to step up to the plate. Iris needs him more than ever, and he has become detached and unfriendly. This whole thing is odd, and I want to have a serious one-on-one with Iris when all of this is over.

I'm pretty bummed out since Jude couldn't make it today. The memorial and wake have been grand, but I have decided to drive down and see him at the stables. I say my farewells to everyone, and head towards Tessentee stables. I pull into the driveway and see his truck parked next to Christina St. Mark's truck. I'm having the terrible gut feeling, but I shake it off. I walk towards the stable and can now hear their voices and conversation. I hear Christina laughing, and I don't think either one has realized that I am here. Jude is always the gentleman. I can't help but think how striking he is and how lucky I am to have him in my life.

As I get closer to where they are standing Jude notices me out of the corner of his eye. "Sonny, you're here!"

Christina is abruptly reserved and restrained.

I greet her in kindness. "Am I interrupting?"

Jude immediately drops what he's doing and greets me with a kiss. I notice Christina, and she definitely seems annoyed with my sudden unexpected arrival. I look at her and think, "Lady, he's taken!"

Her quiet sneer tells me everything I needed to know about Dr. Christina St. Mark. I have a hard time concentrating on Jude's warm welcome. My mind is racing all over the place, but most of all I'm fuming inside. I smile at Jude and put my arms around his waist. He is excited to see me, and that's all that matters. I melt when he smiles great big, and his dimples are incredibly sexy. I have never been so jealous in my entire life, and I hate it. This sudden blow to my self-esteem is killing me. It's a huge distraction, and I'm angry with myself for harboring these feelings.

Jude perceives my attention is elsewhere. "Sonny, tell me about Margaret's funeral."

I glance at him and halfheartedly smile. "You know I'm a straight up person. Do I have to worry about Christina St. Mark?"

He laughs. "Lil' lady, I assure you there ain't nothing goin' on with Dr. St. Mark and me." He picks me up and swings me around. My fears are melted away and completely diminished. Christina, on the other hand, is someone to watch, but right now I'm too happy to worry about it.

"Jude, you are a good man. I truly believe that."

Margaret's funeral may have been a downer, but Jude always makes me feel full of life. He hushes down any concern or fear I may have.

An ol' girlfriend of Margaret is now Iris's pen pal, and she is findin' out a lot of new information about her mother. Iris writes letters to her daily with new questions or thoughts. The return letters are a wealth of information and comfort. Patricia Kay is her name, and she is the only genuine link to Margaret that Iris has been able to find so far. She pens Iris beautiful letters "Your mother and my friend Margaret loved you so very much. Margaret kept her pregnancy with you a secret from her late husband, your father. Steven and Iris's father was a bad alcoholic, and a very physically abusive man. Margaret knew in her heart that she couldn't raise another innocent child by this man. She was desperate and pregnant, but most importantly Margaret had to protect the unborn baby she carried, you." Margaret took extraordinary measures to keep her pregnancy a secret from everybody but Patricia. At that time Patricia Kay was her only friend and confidant.

It was with her help that Margaret was able to make all the arrangements for the private adoption by a family of Margaret's choosing. Patricia told Iris, "The family was solid and good. She goes onto write. "Margaret did ask for help from the police. Back then there wasn't much said or done about violence against women, and divorce was not a religious option for Margaret. Her husband would have to have done grave bodily harm to Margaret before the police could do anything to help her. It was a different time, and now women are starting to come out of the shadows of abuse."

Patricia concludes in her letters, "Your mother had a sad life growing up, and she herself had been physically and sexually abused by her own father. The wonderful news is that Margaret took Steven and got away from her husband a few years after you were adopted. She goes on to close. "I lost touch with Margaret after that, but I've often thought about her over the years. I am proud that Margaret was able to rise above it all, become a successful woman, seek out you, and own a little piece of heaven before she died." Patrica and Iris vow to meet in the future, but the letters offer Iris exactly what she needs right now. I know she will heal over time, and for the very first time in her life she feels loved by her mother. "My mom painstakingly made arrangements for me to be adopted by a good family." The dark unknown details and secrets are slowly coming to light. Iris still has to find out what happened to Margaret after Patricia lost contact with her. It's still a mystery for now, but it's a grand start.

"Iris, I'm so happy for you. I think things are gonna work out for all of us after all." Iris has lived a difficult life, and findin' her mother and brother all at once has to be overwhelming. She always manages to find the good and kind in everything, and she is also the first to admit, "Like Stash always says, crap happens!"

There's a break in the weather, and hopefully spring is around the corner. The last few weeks of winter have been pleasant and peaceful. Stash and Fish hang out a lot since Margaret and Hank are gone. Fish has been helping on his cabin, and they are in the very last stretch of finishing Stash's log cabin. Fish has several months off from touring, and they have put a huge dent into the cabin's completion. Stash has quit drinking for now. I hope and pray this will be the time, and he is able to actually quit. The cabin has been his saving grace, and we all try to lend him a hand when we can. Iris hasn't heard from Steven Beck since he left, and she is starting to find peace with her birth mother.

Peter is coming around, and acting like the man I have always known him to be. It won't be long before they can look at each with the same old passion. This winter has been hard for both of them. Peter has made several suggestions about what to do with Margaret's house, but the one that struck Iris's attention and agreement is a temporary sanctuary for abused women and their children. Iris and Peter couldn't be happier with their decision. It will help abused women and children get back on their feet and away from damaging and dangerous relationships. Margaret's home is paid for, and her retirement pension will pay for the cost of the private lodge.

All the folks at Why Worry embrace the notion, and everyone in the gap will volunteer to work there. Iris may never know why Margaret Beck preferred to keep her true identity a secret, but her legacy lives on through all of the families of domestic violence she will be helping.

Spring is here, and everyone is coming out of their hibernation. The birds are back, and White Rock Mountain is starting to come alive. I can hear the music coming down the holler from Why Worry again, and life moves forward. Iris has named her mom's log cabin, "The Sunshine House." A fitting name for a beautiful place. The shelter will be open soon, and knowing Iris, it will be the perfect healing retriet for many years to come. My desire to write is renewed, and the typewriter is my new best friend. I've learned a lot of lessons over the last year. I learned at the moment of birth life is no longer an option. Strength, courage, and resolve are all you need. Rejoice and celebrate if you are lucky enough to find someone extraordinary, and however you can find love is a beautiful thing. Hate is easy, love is life changing, but death is profound and everlasting. God's grace and Jude's love drench my soul every second I continue to exist.

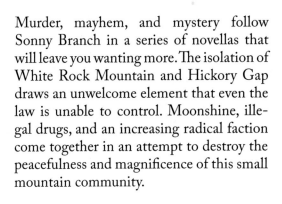

Murder, mayhem, and mystery follow Sonny Branch in a series of novellas that will leave you wanting more. The isolation of White Rock Mountain and Hickory Gap draws an unwelcome element that even the law is unable to control. Moonshine, illegal drugs, and an increasing radical faction come together in an attempt to destroy the peacefulness and magnificence of this small mountain community.